THEY WALKED
LIKE MEN

THEY WALKED
LIKE MEN

CLIFFORD D. SIMAK

OPEN ROAD

INTEGRATED MEDIA

NEW YORK

ISBN: 978-1-5040-7982-2

This edition published in 2023 by Open Road Integrated Media, Inc.
180 Maiden Lane
New York, NY 10038
www.openroadmedia.com

THEY WALKED LIKE MEN

1

It was Thursday night and I'd had too much to drink and the hall was dark and that was the only thing that saved me. If I hadn't stopped beneath the hall light just outside my door to sort out the keys, I would have stepped into the trap, just as sure as hell.

Its being Thursday night had nothing to do with it, actually, but that's the way I write. I'm a newspaperman, and newspapermen put the day of the week and the time of day and all the other pertinent information into everything they write.

The hall was dark because Old George Weber was a penny-pinching soul. He spent half his time fighting with the other tenants about cutting down the heat or not installing air conditioning or the plumbing's being on the fritz again or why he never got around to redecorating. He never fought with me because I didn't care. It was a place to sleep and eat occasionally and to spend what spare time I had, and I wasn't fussy. We thought an awful lot of one another, did Old George and I. We played pinochle together and we drank beer together and every fall we went out to South Dakota for the pheasant hunting. But we wouldn't be going this year, I remembered, because that very morning I had driven Old George and Mrs. George out to the airport and had seen them off on a trip to California. And even if Old George had stayed at home, we wouldn't have been going, for next week I'd be off on the trip the Old Man had been after me to make for the last six months.

I was fumbling for the keys and I was none too steady-handed, for Gavin Walker, the city editor, and I had got into an argument about should science writers be required to cover stuff like council meetings and P.T.A.'s and such. Gavin said that they should and I said that they shouldn't, and first he'd buy some drinks and then I would buy some drinks, until it came closing time and Ed, the bartender, had to throw us out. I'd wondered, when I left the place, if I should risk driving home or maybe call a cab. I had decided finally that probably I could drive, but I took the back streets, where it was unlikely there'd be any cops. I'd got home all right and had got the car maneuvered into the lot back of the apartment building, but I hadn't tried to park it. I'd just left it sitting out in the center of the lot. I was having a hard time getting the right key. They all seemed to look alike, and while I was fumbling them around they slipped out of my fingers and fell onto the carpeting.

I bent down to pick them up and I missed them on the first swipe and I missed them on the second, so I got down on my knees to make a new approach to them.

And it was then I saw it.

Consider this: If Old George had not been a tight man with the buck, he'd put in bigger lights out there in the hall, so that one could walk right up to his door and pick out his key instead of going over to the center of the hall and fumbling around underneath that misplaced lightning bug that functioned as a light bulb. And if I hadn't gotten into the argument with Gavin and taken on a load, I'd never have dropped the keys to start with. And even if I had, I probably could have picked them up without getting on my knees. And if I hadn't gotten on my knees, I never would have seen that the carpeting was cut.

Not torn, you understand. Not worn out. But cut. And cut in a funny way—cut in a semicircle in front of my door. As if someone had used the center of my door as a focal point and, with a knife tied to a three-foot string, had cut a semicircle from the rug. Had cut it and left it there—for the rug had not been taken. Someone had cut a semicircular chunk out of it and then had left it there.

And that, I told myself, was a damn funny thing to do—a senseless sort of thing. For why should anyone want a piece of carpeting cut in that particular shape? And if, for some unfathomable reason, someone had wanted it, why had he cut it out, then left it lying there?

I put out a cautious finger to be sure that I was right—that I wasn't seeing things. And I was right, except it wasn't carpet. The stuff that lay inside that three-foot semicircle looked for all the world like the other carpeting, but it wasn't carpeting. It was some sort of paper—the thinnest sort of paper—that looked exactly like the carpeting.

I pulled back my hand and stayed there on my knees, and I wasn't thinking so much of the cutout carpeting and the paper that was there as I was thinking how I'd explain being on my knees if someone in one of those other apartments should come out in the hall.

But no one came out. The hall stayed empty and it had that musty smell one associates with apartment halls. Above me I heard the tiny singing of the tiny light bulb and I knew by the singing that it was on the verge of burning out. And the new caretaker maybe would replace it with a bigger light bulb. Although, I told myself on second thought, that was most unlikely, for Old George probably had briefed him in minute detail on economic maintenance.

I put out my hand once more and touched the paper with a fingertip, and it was paper—just as I had thought it was—or, at least, it felt very much like paper.

And the idea of that cutout carpeting and the paper in its place made me sore as hell. It was a dirty trick and it was a dirty fraud and I grabbed the paper and jerked it out of there.

Underneath the paper was the trap.

I staggered to my feet, with the paper still hanging from my fingers, and stared at the trap.

I didn't believe it. No man in his right mind would have. People just simply don't go around setting traps for other people—as if those other people might be a bear or fox.

But the trap stayed there, lying on the floor exposed by the cut-out carpeting and until this moment covered by the paper, just as a human trapper would cover his trap with a light sprinkling of leaves or grass to conceal it from his quarry.

It was a big steel trap. I had never seen a bear trap, but I imagine it was as big or bigger than a bear trap. It was a human trap, I told myself, for it had been set for humans. For one human in particular. For there was no doubt it had been set for me.

I backed away from it until I bumped into the wall. I stayed there against the wall, looking at the trap, and on the carpeting between myself and the trap lay the bunch of keys I'd dropped.

It was a gag, I told myself. But I was wrong, of course. It wasn't any gag. If I'd stepped over to the door instead of stopping underneath the light, it would have been no gag. I'd have a mangled leg—or perhaps both legs mangled and perhaps some broken bones—for the jaws were equipped with jagged, offset teeth. And no one in God's world could have forced the jaws apart once they'd snapped upon their victim. To free a man from a trap like that would call for wrenches to take the trap apart.

I shivered, thinking of it. A man could bleed to death before anyone could get that trap apart.

I stood there, looking at the trap, with my hand crumpling up the paper as I looked. And then I raised an arm and hurled the wad of paper at the trap. It hit one jaw and rolled off and barely missed the pan and lay there between the jaws.

I'd have to get a stick or something, I told myself, and spring the trap before I could get into my place. I could call the cops, of course, but there'd be no sense in that. They'd create a terrible uproar and more than likely take me down to head-quarters to ask me a lot of questions, and I didn't have the time. I was all tuckered out and all I wanted was to crawl into my bed.

More than that, a ruckus of that sort would give the apartment a bad name, and that would be a dirty trick to play on Old George when he was out in California. And it would give all my neighbors something to talk about and they'd want to talk to me about it and I didn't want that. They left me alone and that was the way I wanted it. I was happy just the way it was.

I wondered where I could find a stick, and the only place I could think of was the closet down on the first floor where the brooms and mops and the vacuum cleaner and the other junk were kept. I tried to remember if the closet might be locked, and I didn't think it was, but I couldn't be positively sure.

I stepped out from the wall and started for the stairs. I had just reached the top of them when something made me turn around. I don't think I heard anything. I'm fairly sure I didn't. But the effect was the same as if I had.

There was something said for me to turn around, and I turned around so fast my feet got tangled up and threw me to the floor.

And even as I fell I saw the trap was wilting.

I tried to ease my fall by putting out my hands, but I didn't do so well. I hit with quite a thud and banged my head, and my brain was full of stars.

I got my hands under me and hoisted up my front and shook the stars away and the trap had gone on wilting.

The jaws were limp and the whole contraption was humped up in a most peculiar way. I watched it in some wonder, not doing anything, just lying there, with the front of me propped up on my arms.

The trap got limper and limper and began to hump together. It was as if a piece of mashed-out, mangled plastic putty was trying to put itself into shape again. And it did put itself into shape. It made itself into a ball. All this time that it has been humping itself together, it had been changing color, and when it finally was a ball it was as black as pitch.

It lay there for a moment in front of the door and then it began rolling slowly, as if it took a lot of effort to get itself to rolling.

And it rolled straight for me!

I tried to get out of its way, but it built its speed up fast and I thought for an instant it would crash straight into me. It was about the size of a bowling ball, maybe just a little bigger, and I had no way of knowing how heavy it might be.

But it didn't hit me. It brushed me, that was all.

I twisted to watch it go down the stairs, and that was a funny thing. It bounced down the steps, but not the way a normal ball would bounce. It bounced short and fast, not high and lazy—as if there were a law which said it must hit every tread but make the best speed that it could. It went down the flight, hitting every tread, and it went around the corner post so fast you could almost see the smoke.

I scrambled to my feet and got to the banister and leaned over to see the flight below. But the ball was out of sight. There was no sign of it.

I went back down the hall and there, underneath the light, lay the bunch of keys, and there was the three-foot semicircle cut out of the carpet.

I got down on my knees and picked up the keys and found the right one finally and got over to the door. I unlocked it and went into the apartment and locked the door, real fast, behind me before I even took the time to turn on a light.

I got the light turned on and made it to the kitchen. I sat down at the breakfast table and remembered there was a pitcher almost half full of tomato juice in the refrigerator and that I should drink some of it. But I couldn't stand the thought of it. I gagged just thinking of it. What I really needed was another slug of booze, but I'd had too much of that already.

I sat there, thinking about the trap and why anyone would set a trap for me. It was the craziest thing I had ever heard of. If I hadn't seen that trap myself, I'd never have believed it.

It was no trap, of course—no regular trap, that is. For regular traps do not wilt and roll into a ball and go rolling away when they've failed to catch their quarry.

I tried to reason it all out, but my brain was fuzzy and I was sleepy and I was safe at home and tomorrow was another day. So I gave up everything and staggered off to bed.

2

Something jerked me out of sleep.

I came up straight, not knowing where I was, not knowing who I was—entirely disoriented, not fuzzy, not sleepy, not confused, but with that terrible, cold clarity of mind that makes an emptiness of everything in its sudden flash of being.

I was in a silence, in an emptiness, in a lightless nowhere, and that clear, cold mind speared out like a striking snake, seeking, finding nothing, and horrified at the nothingness.

Then the clamor came—the high, shrill, insistent, insane clamor, which was entirely mindless in that it was not meant for me or for anything but clamored solely for itself.

The silence fell again and there were shadows that were shapes—a square of half-light that turned out to be a window, a faint gleam from the kitchen where the light still burned, a crouched, dark monstrosity that was an easy chair.

The phone screamed again through the morning darkness and I tumbled out of bed, heading blindly for a door that I could not see. Groping, I found it, and the phone was silent now.

I went across the living room, stumbling in the darkness, and was putting out my hand when it began to ring again.

I jerked it from the cradle viciously and mumbled into it.

There was something the matter with my tongue. It didn't want to work.

"Parker?"

"Who else?"

"This is Joe—Joe Newman."

"Joe?" Then I remembered. Joe Newman was the dogwatch man on the night desk at the paper.

"Hate to get you up," said Joe.

I mumbled at him wrathfully.

"Something funny happened. Thought you ought to know."

"Look, Joe," I said. "Call Gavin. He's the city editor. He gets paid for being gotten out of bed."

"But this is down your alley, Parker. This is—"

"Yeah, I know," I told him. "A flying saucer landed."

"Not that. You ever hear of Timber Lane?"

"Out by the lake," I said. "Way out west of town."

"That's it. The old Belmont place is at the end of it. House closed up. Ever since the Belmont family moved out to Arizona. Kids use the road as a lovers' lane."

"Now, look, Joe . . ."

"I was getting to it, Parker. Some kids were parked out there tonight. They saw a bunch of balls rolling down the road. Like bowling balls, one behind the other."

I'm afraid I yelled at him: "They what?"

"They saw these things in the headlights when they were driving out and got panicky. Put a call in to the cops."

I got myself in hand and made my voice calm. "Cops find anything?"

"Just tracks," said Joe.

"Bowling ball tracks?"

"Yeah, I guess you could call them that."

I told him: "Kids been drinking, maybe."

"Cops didn't say so. They talked with these kids. They just saw the balls rolling down the road. They didn't stop to investigate. They just got out of there."

I didn't say anything. I was trying to figure out what I ought to say. And I was scared. Scared stiff.

"What do you think of it, Parker?"

"I don't know," I said. "Imagination maybe. Or ribbing the cops."

"The cops found tracks."

"Kids could have made them. Could have rolled some bowling balls up and down the road, picking out the dusty places. Figured they'd get their names into the papers. They get bored and crazy . . ."

"You wouldn't use it, then?"

"Look, Joe—I'm not the city editor. It's not up to me. Ask Gavin. He's the man who decides what we publish."

"And you don't think there's anything to it? Maybe it's a hoax?"

"How the hell would I know?" I yelled at him.

He got sore at me. I don't blame him much.

"Thanks, Parker. Sorry that I troubled you," he said, and then hung up, and the phone began its steady drone.

"Good night, Joe," I said into the drone. "I'm sorry that I yelled."

It helped, saying it, even if he wasn't there to hear.

And I wondered why I'd tried to downgrade the story, why I'd tried to suggest it was no more than some teen-age prank.

Because, you slob, you're scared, said that inner man who sometimes talks to you. Because you'd give almost anything to make yourself believe there is nothing to it. Because you don't want to be reminded of that trap out in the hall.

I put the receiver back into the cradle, and my hand was shaking, so that it made a clatter when I put it down.

I stood in the darkness and felt the terror closing in. And when I tried to put a finger on the terror, there was nothing there. For it wasn't terrible; it was comic—a trap set outside a door, a pack of bowling balls trundling sedately down a country lane. It was the stuff cartoons are made of. It was something that was too ridiculous to believe. It was something that would send you off into helpless guffaws even as it killed you.

If it meant to kill.

And that was the question, certainly. Was it meant to kill?

Had that trap outside the door actually been a trap, made of honest steel or its equivalent? Or had it been a toy, made of harmless plastic or its equivalent?

And the hardest question of them all—had it actually been there? I knew it had, of course. For I had seen it there. But my mind kept trying to reject it. For my comfort and my sanity, my mind pushed it away and the logic in me screamed against the very thought of it.

I had been drunk, of course, but not as drunk as that. Not falling-down drunk, not seeing-things drunk—just a little shaky in the hands and weakish in the knees.

Now I was all right—except for that terrible, lonely coldness of the mind. Type three hangover—and, in many ways, the worst of all of them.

By now my eyes had become somewhat dark-adapted and I could make out the formless shape of furniture. I made my way to the kitchen without stumbling over anything. The door was open a crack and a shaft of light streamed through.

I had left the ceiling light on when I'd gone pottering off to bed, and the clock on the wall said it was three-thirty.

I discovered that I was still better than half dressed and rather badly rumpled. My shoes were off and my tie was untied but still trailing from the collar, and I was a mess.

I stood there, taking counsel with myself. If I went back to bed at this hour of the morning, I'd sleep like a sodden lump until noon or better and wake up feeling terrible.

But if I got cleaned up now and got some food inside of me and went to the office early, before anyone else arrived, I'd get a lot of work done and could knock off early in the day and have a decent weekend.

And it was a Friday and I had a date with Joy. I stood there for a while without doing anything, feeling good about Friday night and Joy.

I planned it all—there'd just be time to boil the coffee water while I took a shower, and I'd have toast and eggs and bacon and I'd drink a lot of tomato juice, which might do something for the lonely coldness of the mind.

But first of all, before I did anything at all, I'd look out in the hall and see if the semicircle still was gone from the carpeting.

I went to the door and looked.

In front of it lay the preposterous semicircle of bare flooring.

I jeered thinly at my doubting mind and my outraged logic and went back into the kitchen to put on the coffee water.

3

A newsroom is a cold and lonely place early in the morning. It is big and empty, and it's neat, so neat that it is depressing. Later in the day it takes on the clutter that makes it warm and human—the clipped, dismembered papers littered on the desks, the balls of scrunched-up copy paper tossed onto the floor, the overflowing spikes. But in the morning, after the maintenance crew has it tidied up, it has something of the pallor of an operating room. The few lights that are burning seem far too bright and the stripped-down desks and chairs so precisely placed that they spell a hard efficiency—the efficiency that later in the day is masked and softened when the staff is hard at work and the place is littered and that strange undertone of bedlam which goes into each edition of the paper is building to a peak.

The morning staff had gone home hours before and Joe Newman also was gone. I had rather expected that I might find him there, but his desk was as straight and neat as all the rest of them and there was no sign of him.

The pastepots, all freshly scraped and cleaned and filled with fresh, new paste, stood in solemn, shiny rows upon the city and the copydesks. Each pot was adorned with a brush thrust into the paste at a jaunty angle. The copy off the wire machines was laid out precisely on the news desk. And from the cubby hole over in the corner came the muted chuckle of the wire machines themselves, busily grinding out the grist of news from all parts of the world.

Somewhere in the tangled depths of the half-dark newsroom a copyboy was whistling—one of those high-pitched, jerky tunes that are no tunes at all. I shuddered at the sound of it. There was something that was almost obscene about someone whistling at this hour of the morning.

I went over to my desk and sat down. Someone on the maintenance crew had taken all my magazines and scientific journals and stacked them in a pile. Only the afternoon before, I'd gone through them carefully and set aside the ones I would be using in getting out my columns. I looked sourly at the stack and swore. Now I'd have to paw through all of them to find the ones I wanted.

A copy of the last edition of the morning paper lay white and naked on the clean desk top. I picked it up and leaned back in the chair and began running through the news.

There wasn't much of anything. There still was trouble down in Africa, and the Venezuela mess was looking fairly nasty. Someone had held up a downtown drugstore just before closing time, and there was a picture of a buck-toothed clerk pointing out to a bored policeman where the holdup man had stood. The governor had said that the legislature, when it came back next year, would have to buckle down to its responsibility of finding some new sources of tax revenue. If this wasn't done, said the governor, the state would be going down the drain. It was something that the governor had said many times before.

Over in the top, left-hand corner of page one was an area economic roundup by-lined by Grant Jensen, business editor of the morning staff. Grant was in one of his professionally optimistic moods. The upward business trend, he wrote, was running strong and steady. Store sales were holding well, industrial indexes all were on the up side, there was no immediate prospect of any labor trouble—things were looking rosy. This was especially true, the article went on to say, in the home construction field. The demand for housing had outrun supply, and all the home builders in the entire federal reserve district were booked to full capacity for almost a year ahead.

I am afraid I yawned. It all was true, undoubtedly, but it still was the same old crud that jerks like Jensen were forever handing out. But the publisher would like it, for it made the advertisers feel just fine and it promoted boom psychology, and the old war-horses of the financial district would talk about the piece that had been in the morning paper when they went to lunch this noon at the Union Club.

Let it run the other way, I told myself—let the store sales drop off, let the housing boom go bust, let factories start to turn away their workers—and until the situation became inescapable, there'd be not a word about it.

I folded the paper and put it to one side. Opening up a drawer, I got out a batch of notes I'd made the afternoon before and started going through them.

Lightning, the early-morning copyboy, came out of the shadows and stood beside my desk.

"Good morning, Mr. Graves," he said.

"Was that you whistling?" I asked.

"Yeah, I guess it was."

He laid a proof on my desk.

"Your column for today," he said. "The one about how come the mammoth and all those other big animals happened to die out. I thought you'd like to see it."

I picked it up and looked at it. As usual, some joker on the copydesk had written a smart-aleck headline for it.

"You're in early, Mr. Graves," said Lightning.

I explained: "I have to get my columns out for a couple of weeks ahead. I'll be going on a trip."

"I heard about it," said Lightning eagerly. "Astronomy."

"Well, yes, I guess you could say that. All the big observatories. Have to write a series about outer space. Way out. Galaxies and stuff."

"Mr. Graves," said Lightning, "do you think maybe they'll let you look through some of the telescopes?"

"I doubt it. Telescope time is pretty tightly scheduled."

"Mr. Graves . . ."

"What is it, Lightning?"

"You think there are people out there? Out on them other stars?"

"I wouldn't know. No one knows. It stands to reason there must be other life somewhere."

"Like us?"

"No, I don't think like us."

Lightning stood there, shuffling his feet; then he said suddenly: "Gosh, I forgot to tell you, Mr. Graves. There's someone here to see you."

"Someone here?"

"Yeah. He came in a couple of hours ago. I told him you wouldn't be in for a long time yet. But he said he'd wait."

"Where is he, then?"

"He went into the monitoring room and took the easy chair in there. I guess he fell asleep."

I heaved myself out of the chair. "Let's go and see," I said.

I might have known. There was no one else who would do a thing like that. There was no one else to whom the time of day meant nothing.

He lay back in the chair, with a silly smile pasted on his face. From the radio panel issued the low-voiced gabble of the various police departments, the highway patrol, the fire departments, and the other agencies of law and order, forming a background of gibberish for his polite snoring.

We stood and looked at him.

Lightning asked: "Who is he, Mr. Graves? Do you know him, Mr. Graves?"

"His name," I said, "is Carleton Stirling. He's a biologist over at the university and a friend of mine."

"He don't look like no biologist to me," said Lightning firmly.

"Lightning," I told the skeptic, "you will find in time that biologists and astronomers and physicists and all the rest of that ungodly tribe of science are just people like the rest of us."

"But coming in at three o'clock to see you. Expecting you'd be here."

"That's the way he lives," I said. "It wouldn't occur to him that the rest of the world might live differently. That's the kind of man he is."

And that's the kind of man he was, all right.

He owned a watch, but he never used it except to time off the tests and experiments he happened to be doing. He never, actually, knew what time of day it was. When he got hungry, he scrounged up some food. When he couldn't keep awake, he found a place to curl up and hammered off some sleep. When he had finished what he was doing or, maybe, got discouraged, he'd set off for a cabin that he owned on a lake up north and spend a day or week loafing.

He so consistently forgot to go to classes, so seldom turned up for scheduled lectures, that the university administration finally gave up. They no longer even bothered to pretend that he instructed. They let him keep his lab and let him hole up there with his cages of guinea pigs and rats and his apparatus. But they got their money's worth. He was forever coming up with something that spelled publicity—not only for himself but for the university. So far as he, himself, was concerned, the university could have had it all. In the public eye or the public print, or out of it—there was no difference so far as Carleton Stirling was concerned.

The only things he lived for were his experiments, his ceaseless delvings into the mysteries that lay like a challenge to him. He had an apartment, but there were times when he didn't visit it for days. He tossed paychecks into drawers and left them accumulating there until the university's accounting people phoned him urgently to find out what could have happened to them. Once he won a prize—not one of the big, imposing ones, but still one full of honor and with some cash attached—and forgot entirely to attend the dinner where it was to have been awarded to him.

And now he lay back in the chair, with his head rolled against its back and his long legs outthrust into the shadow underneath the radio console. He was snoring gently and he looked not like one of the world's most promising research men but like a transient who might have wandered in to find a place to sleep. He needed not only a shave but a haircut as well. His tie was knotted unevenly and pulled around to one side, and there were spots upon it, more than likely from the cans of soup he had heated up and spooned down absent-mindedly while he continued to wrestle with whatever problem he currently was concerned with.

I stepped into the room and put a hand down on his shoulder and shook him gently.

He came awake easily, not startled, and looked up at me and grinned.

"Hi, Parker," he said to me.

"Hi, yourself," I said. "I would have let you finish out your sleep, but I was afraid you'd break your neck the way you had it twisted."

He uncoiled and got up and followed me out into the newsroom.

"Almost morning," he said, nodding at the windows. "Time to get awake."

I looked and saw that the windows were no longer black but beginning to get gray.

He ran his fingers through his shock of hair, went through the motions of wiping off his face with an open hand. Then he dug into a pocket and brought out a fistful of crumpled bills. He selected two of them and handed them to me.

"Here," he said. "Just happened to remember. Thought I'd better do it before I forgot again."

"But, Carl . . ."

He shook the two bills impatiently, shoving them at me.

"A couple of years ago," he told me. "That weekend up at the lake. I ran out of money playing slot machines."

I took the bills and put them in my pocket. I could just vaguely remember the incident.

"You mean you stopped by just to pay me off?"

"Sure," he said. "Was passing the building and there was a parking place. Thought I'd run up and see you."

"But I don't work at night."

He grinned at me. "Didn't matter, Parker. It got me some sleep."

"I'll stand you breakfast There's a joint across the street Ham and eggs are good."

He shook his head. "Must be getting back. Wasted too much time. I have work to do."

"Something new?" I asked him.

He hesitated for a moment, then he said: "Nothing publishable. Not yet. Maybe later, but not yet. A long way yet to go."

I waited, looking at him.

"Ecology," he said.

"I don't get you."

"You know what ecology is, Parker."

"Sure. The interrelation of life and conditions in a common area."

He asked me: "You ever wonder what kind of life pattern it would take to be independent of all surrounding factors—a non-ecological creature, so to speak?"

"It's impossible," I told him. "There is food and air—"

"Just an idea. Just a hunch. A puzzle, let us say. A conundrum in adaptability. It'll probably come to nothing."

"Just the same, I'll ask you every now and then."

"Do that," he said. "And the next time you come over, remind me about the gun. The one you loaned me to take up to the lake."

He'd borrowed it a month before to do some target shooting when he'd gone up to his cabin. No one in his right mind, no one but Carleton Stirling, would want to do target practice with a .303.

"I used up your box of cartridges," he said. "I bought another box."

"It wasn't necessary."

"Well, hell," he said, "I had a lot of fun."

He didn't say good-bye. He just turned on his heels and strode out of the newsroom and down the corridor. We heard him go clattering down the stairs.

"Mr. Graves," said Lightning, "that guy is plumb nuts."

I didn't answer Lightning. I went back to my desk and tried to get to work.

4

Gavin Walker came in. He pulled out his assignment book and looked at it. He made a disrespectful noise.

"Shorthanded again," he told me bitterly. "Charlie called in sick. Hangover, more than likely. Al is tied up with the Melburn case down in district court. Bert is trying to finish up that series of his on the freeway progress. The brass is screaming for it. It's overdue right now."

He took off his jacket and hung it on the back of his chair. He threw his hat into a copy basket. He stood there, in the glare of the lights, pugnaciously rolling up his sleeves.

"Someday, by God," he said, "Franklin's will catch fire, jammed with a million shoppers, who turn into a screaming, panic-stricken mob—"

"And you won't have a man to send there."

Gavin blinked at me owlishly. "Parker," he said, "that is exactly it."

It was a favorite speculation of his in moments of great stress. We all knew it by heart.

Franklin's was the city's biggest department store and our best advertising account.

I walked over to the window and looked out. It was beginning to get light outside. The city had that bleak, frosty look of a thing

not quite alive, a sort of sinister fairyland that is on the verge of
winter. A few cars went drifting past in the street below. There was
a pedestrian or two. Scattered early lights burned in the windows of
some of the downtown buildings.

"Parker," said Gavin.

I swung around to face him. "Now, look," I said, "I know you
are shorthanded. But I have work to do. I have a bunch of columns
to get up. I came in early so I could get them done."

"I notice," he said nastily, "you're working hard on them."

"Damn it," I told him, "I have to get woke up."

I went back to my desk and tried to get to work.

Lee Hawkins, the picture editor, came in. He was virtually froth-
ing at the mouth. The color lab had bollixed up the picture for page
one; Foaming threats, he went downstairs to get it straightened out.

Other members of the staff came in and the place took on some
warmth and life. The copy editors began to bawl for Lightning to
go across the street and get their morning coffee. Protesting bitterly,
Lightning went to get it.

I settled down to work. It came easy now. The words rolled out
and the ideas came together. For now there was the atmosphere
for it, the feel for writing—the clamor and the bustle that spelled
newspaper office.

I had one column finished and was starting on the second when
someone stopped beside my desk.

I looked up and saw that it was Dow Crane, a writer on the business desk. I like Dow. He's not a jerk like Jensen. He writes it as he
sees it. He butters up no one. He polishes no apples.

He was looking glum.

I told him that he was.

"I got troubles, Parker."

He pulled out a pack of cigarettes and offered one to me. He
knows that I don't smoke them, but he always offers one. I waved
them off. He lit one for himself.

"You do something for me, maybe?"

I said that I would.

"A man phoned me at home last night. He's coming in this morning. Says he can't find a house."

"What house does he want to find?"

"A house to live in. Almost any house. Says he sold his home three or four months ago and now he can't find one to buy."

"Well, that's tough luck," I said unfeelingly. "What can we do about it?"

"He says he's not the only one. Claims there are a lot of others. Says there isn't a house or apartment to be had in town."

"Dow, the guy is crazy."

"Maybe not," said Dow. "You been looking at the want ads?"

I shook my head. "No reason to," I told him.

"Well, I did. This morning. Column after column of ads by people who want a place to live—any place to live. Some of them sound desperate."

"Jensen's piece this morning . . ."

"You mean about the housing boom?"

"That's it," I said. "It doesn't add up, Dow. Not that piece and what this man was telling you."

"Maybe not. I'm sure it doesn't. But, look, I have to go out to the airport and meet a big wheel who is coming in. It's the only way I can get an interview in time for the first edition. If this guy who phoned me comes in about the house and I'm not here, will you talk to him?"

"Sure thing," I said.

"Thanks," said Dow, and walked off to his desk.

Lightning showed up, carrying the coffee orders in the battered, stained wire service paper box that he kept, when not in use, beneath the picture desk. All hell broke loose immediately. He'd gotten one coffee with cream and no one wanted cream. He'd gotten three with sugar and there were only two men who could drink the stuff with sugar. He'd fouled up on the doughnuts.

I turned back to my machine and got to work again.

The place had hit its normal stride.

Once the daily coffee battle between Lightning and the copy-desk had taken place, one knew the place was grooved, that the newsroom at last had slipped into high gear.

I didn't work for long.

A hand fell on my shoulder.

I looked up and it was Gavin.

"Park, old boy," he said.

"No," I told him sternly.

"You're the only man in the place who can handle this," he told me. "It's Franklin's."

"Don't tell me there's a fire and a million shoppers—"

"No, not that," he said. "Bruce Montgomery just phoned. He's calling a press conference for nine o'clock."

Bruce Montgomery was the president of Franklin's.

"That is Dow's department."

"Dow left for the airport."

I gave up. There was nothing else to do. The guy was practically in tears. I hate city editors who cry.

"All right, then," I said. "I'll be there. What's it all about?"

"I don't know," said Gavin. "I asked Bruce and he wouldn't say. It's bound to be important. Last time they called a press conference was fifteen years ago, when they announced that Bruce was taking over. First time an outsider ever held a top office in the store. It had been all family up till then."

"OK," I said. "I'll take care of it."

He turned around and trotted back to the city desk.

I yelled for a boy and, when one finally showed up, sent him out the library to get me the clips on Franklin's for the last five years or so.

I took the clips out of the envelopes and thumbed through them. There wasn't much in them that I didn't know. Nothing of importance. There were stories about style shows at Franklin's and about art exhibits at Franklin's and about Franklin's personnel taking part in a host of civic endeavors.

Franklin's was an ancient place and tradition-ridden. It had, just the year before, celebrated its hundredth anniversary. It had been a household word almost since the day the city had been founded. It had been (and still was) a family institution, with its precepts fostered as carefully as is possible only in a family institution. Generation after generation had grown up with Franklin's, shopping there almost from the cradle to the grave, and it was a byword for fairness in its dealings and in the quality of its merchandise.

Joy Kane came walking past the desk.

"Hi, beautiful," I said. "What's the deal this morning?"

"Skunks," she said.

"Mink is more your style."

She stopped and stood close beside me. I could smell just the faintest hint of some perfume that she was wearing and, more than that, I could feel the presence of her beauty.

She put out a hand and ruffled my hair, just a quick, impulsive move, and then she was proper once again.

"Tame skunks," she said. "Pet skunks. They are the newest thing. Deodorized, of course."

"Naturally," I said. And I was thinking—cute and hydrophobia.

"I was sore at Gavin when he chased me out there."

"Out into the woods?"

"No. Out to this skunk farm."

"You mean they raise them just like pigs and chickens?"

"Certainly they do. I was telling you these skunks are pets. This man says they make the swellest pets. Clean and cuddly and a lot of fun. He's getting stacks of orders for them. Pet dealers in New York and Chicago and a lot of other places."

"I suppose that you have pictures."

"Ben went out with me. He took a lot of them."

"Where does this man get his skunks?"

"I told you. He raises them."

"To start with, I mean."

"Trappers. Farm boys. He pays good prices for the wild ones. He's building up his business. He needs wild breeding stock. He'll buy all that he can get."

"Which reminds me," I told her. "Payday today. You're going to help me spend the check?"

She said, "Certainly I am. Don't you remember that you asked me?"

"There's a new joint opening out on Pinecrest Drive."

"That sound like fun," she said.

"Seven?"

"Not a minute later. I get hungry early."

She went on to her desk and I went back to the clips. But even on a second look there was nothing in them. I shuffled them together and put them back into the envelopes.

I sat back in my chair and thought about skunks and hydrophobia and the crazy things that some people do.

5

The man who sat at the head of the table beside Bruce Montgomery was bald—aggressively bald, as if he took a pride in baldness, so completely bald that I found myself wondering if he'd ever grown hair. There was a fly crawling on his head and he paid no attention to it. It made me cringe just to watch that fly, walking jauntily and unconcerned across the pinkness of the naked scalp. I could almost feel the slow and maddening prickliness as it pranced along its way.

But the man sat there, unconcerned, not looking at us but staring out above our heads, as if there were something on the rear wall of the conference room that fascinated him. So far as he seemed to be concerned, we weren't even there. He was impersonal and had a touch of coldness, and he never moved. If you hadn't noticed he was breathing, you would have been convinced that Bruce had hauled one of the window mannequins into the room and set it at the table.

The fly walked over the dome of baldness and disappeared from view, crawling out of sight down the rear exposure of that shining skull.

The television boys still were fiddling around with their equipment, getting it set up, and Bruce glanced at them with some impatience.

The room was fairly well filled up. There were the television and the radio people and the AP and UPI reporters and the man who was a stringer for the *Wall Street Journal.*

Bruce looked over at the TV setups once again. "Everybody set?" he asked.

"Just a minute, Bruce," said one of the TV crowd.

So we waited while the cameras were adjusted and the cords were strung and the technicians messed around. That's the way it goes with these TV jerks. They insist on being in on everything and scream if you leave them out, but let them in and they bollix up the detail beyond all imagination. They have the place all cluttered up and you have to wait for them and they take a lot of time.

I sat there and, for some reason, got to thinking about all the fun Joy and I had had the last few months. We'd gone on picnics and we'd gone fishing and she was one of the finest gals I had ever known. She was a good newspaperwoman, but in becoming a newspaperwoman she had stayed a woman, and that's not always true. Too many of them think they have to get rough and tough to uphold tradition, and that, of course, is a total canard. Newspapermen never were as rough and tough as the movies tried to make them. They are just a bunch of hardworking specialists who do the best they can.

The fly came crawling back over the horizon of the gleaming skull. It stood on the skyline for a moment, then tipped up on its head and brushed its wings with its rearward pair of feet. It stayed there for a while, looking the situation over, then wheeled around and went back out of sight.

Bruce tapped the table with his pencil.

"Gentlemen," he said.

The room became so quiet that I could hear the breathing of the man who was sitting next to me.

And in that moment while we waited I sensed again the depth of that dignity and decorum which was implicit in this room, with its thick carpeting and its richly paneled walls, the heavy draperies and the pair of paintings on the wall behind the table.

Here, I thought, was the epitome of the Franklin family and the store that it had built, the position that it held and what it meant to this certain city. Here was the dignity and the foursquare virtue, here the civic spirit and the cultural standard.

"Gentlemen," said Bruce, "there is no use employing a lot of preliminaries. Something has happened that, a month ago, I would have said never could have happened. I'll tell you and then you can ask your questions . . ."

He stopped talking for a moment, as if he might be searching for the proper words. He halted in the middle of his sentence and he did not drop his voice. His face was bleak and white.

Then he said it slowly and concisely: "Franklin's has been sold."

We sat silent for a moment, every man of us, not stunned, not stricken, but completely unbelieving. For of all the things that one might have conjured up in his imagining, this was the last thing that any of us would have hit upon. For Franklin's, and the Franklin family, was a tradition in the town. It, and the family, had been there almost as long as the town had been. To sell Franklin's was like selling the courthouse or a church.

Bruce's face was hard and expressionless and I wondered how he could have said the words, for Bruce Montgomery was as much a part of Franklin's as the Franklin family—probably in these later years more a part of it, for he'd managed it and coddled it and worried over it for more years than most of us could readily recall.

Then the silence broke and the questions came, all of them at once.

Bruce waved us all to silence.

"Not me," he told us. "Mr. Bennett will answer all your questions."

The bald man for the first time now took notice of us. He lowered his eyes from the spot on the back wall of the room. He nodded slightly at us.

"One at a time, if you please," he said.

"Mr. Bennett," asked someone from the back of the room, "are you the new owner?"

"No. I simply represent the owner."

"Who is the owner, then?"

"That is something I can't tell you," Bennett said.

"You mean that you don't know who the owner is, or—"

"It means that I can't tell you."

"Could you tell us the consideration?"

"You mean, of course, how much was paid for it."

"Yes, that is—"

"That, too," said Bennett, "is not for publication."

"Bruce," said a disgusted voice.

Montgomery shook his head. "Mr. Bennett, please," he said. "He will answer all your questions."

"Can you tell us," I asked Bennett, "what the new owner's policy may be? Will the store continue as it has before? Will the same policies as to quality and credit and civic—"

"The store," said Bennett flatly, "will be closed."

"You mean for reorganization . . ."

"Young man," said Bennett, clipping off his words, "I don't mean that at all. The store will be closed. It will not reopen. There will be no Franklin's. Not any more, there won't."

I caught a glimpse of Bruce Montgomery's face. If I live to be a million, I'll never erase from memory the shock and surprise and anguish that was on his face.

6

I was finishing the last page of the story, with Gavin hovering over me, breathing down my neck, and the copydesk a-howl that it was way past deadline, when the publisher's secretary phoned.

"Mr. Maynard would like to talk with you," she told me, "as soon as you are free."

"Almost immediately," I said, hanging up the phone.

I finished the final paragraph and whipped out the sheet. Gavin grabbed it and rushed it to the copydesk.

He came back to me again. He nodded at the phone.

"The Old Man?" he asked.

I said it had been. "He wants to ask me all about it, I suppose. Another third degree."

It was a way the Old Man had. Not that he didn't trust us. Not that he thought we were goofing off or holding back on anything or distorting anything. It was the newspaperman in him, I'd guess—the screaming need for detail, hoping that by talking with us he might discover some angle we had missed, a raking over of the gravel of raw facts in a maddening look for gold. I suppose it made him feel he was keeping his hand in.

"It's a terrible blow," said Gavin. "There goes a fat contract. The boy down in advertising who was handling the account probably is off in some dark corner cutting his throat."

"Not only tough for us," I said. "Tough for the entire town."

For Franklin's was not a shopping center only; it was likewise an unofficial social center. Old ladies, with their neatly tailored suits and their prim and careful coiffures, made a quiet and regular celebration in the tearoom on the seventh floor. Housewives out for a day of shopping invariably would meet old friends at Franklin's— likewise on a shopping mission—and would block the aisles with impromptu reunions. People were always meeting other people there by prearranged appointment. And there were the art shows and the uplift lectures and all the other trappings that are the hallmark of genteel America. Franklin's was a marketplace and a rendezvous and a sort of club for the people of all classes and all walks of life.

I got up from my desk and went down the corridor to the boss's office.

His name is William Woodruff Maynard and he is not a bad guy. Not nearly so bad as the name would make you think.

Charlie Gunderson, who headed up retail advertising, was in the office with him, and the both of them looked worried.

The Old Man offered me a cigar out of the big box that stood on the corner of his desk, but I refused it and sat down in a chair alongside Charlie, facing the Old Man, who sat behind the desk.

"I phoned Bruce," the Old Man said, "and he was noncommittal. I might even say evasive. He doesn't want to talk."

"I don't imagine that he does," I said. "I think it was as great a shock to him as to the rest of us."

"I don't understand you, Parker. Why should it be a shock? He must have been the one who negotiated and arranged the sale."

"The closing of the store," I explained. "That's what we are talking about, I take it. I don't think Bruce knew the new owner planned to close the store. I think if he'd suspected that, there would have been no sale."

"What makes you think that, Parker?"

"The look on Bruce's face," I told him. "When Bennett said they'd close down the store. Surprised and shocked and angry and, perhaps, a little sick. Like a man whose four kings bump up against four aces."

"But he said nothing."

"What was there for him to say? He had closed the deal and the store was sold. I don't imagine it ever crossed his mind that someone would buy a prosperous business and then simply close it down."

"No," said the Old Man thoughtfully, "it doesn't make much sense."

"It might be just a publicity gag," said Charlie Gunderson. "Just a public come-on. You'll have to admit that never in its history has Franklin's ever gotten the publicity it is getting now."

"Franklin's," said the Old Man stiffly, "never sought publicity. They didn't need publicity."

"In just a day or two," persisted Charlie, "there'll be a big announcement the store is opening up again. The new management will say they're giving in to the public clamor that Franklin's should go on."

"I don't think so," I said, and realized immediately that I should have kept my mouth shut. For I didn't have a thing to go on, just a sort of hunch. The whole deal smelled. There was more to it, I could have sworn, than just a gag some publicity man had thought up in an idle moment.

But they didn't ask me, either one of them, why I thought it was no gag.

"Parker," said the Old Man, "you have no inkling at all as to who's behind this deal?"

I shook my head. "Bennett wasn't saying. The store had been purchased—building, stock, goodwill, everything—by the man, or men, he was representing, and it is being closed. No reason for its being closed. No plans to use the building for something else."

"I imagine he was questioned rather closely."

I nodded.

"And he wasn't talking?"

"Not a word," I said.

"Strange," the Old Man said. "It's most devilish strange."

"This Bennett?" asked Charlie. "What do you know about him?"

"Nothing. He refused to identify himself except as the agent of the buyer."

"You tried, of course," the Old Man said.

"Not me. I had to write the story to catch the first edition and there was only twenty minutes. Gavin has a couple of people checking the hotels."

"I'll lay you twenty dollars," the Old Man offered, "they'll find no trace of him."

I suppose I looked surprised.

"It's a funny business," the Old Man said, "from the first to last. A negotiation such as this is most difficult to keep entirely under cover. And yet there was no leak, no rumor, not a breath of it."

"If there had been," I pointed out. "Dow would have known about it. And if he'd known about it, he'd been working on it, instead of going to the airport. . . ."

"I quite agree with you," the Old Man said. "Dow knows the most of everything that's going on downtown."

"Was there anything about this Bennett," Charlie asked me "that might give you a clue—any kind of clue?"

I shook my head. All I could remember of him was the total baldness of his head and the fly crawling on that baldness and his paying no attention to it.

"Well, thank you, Parker," said the Old Man. "I would imagine you did your usual job. Highly competent. With men like you and Dow and Gavin out there in the city room we don't have any worries."

I got out of there before he broke down to the point where he might have tried to raise my salary. That would have been an awful thing.

I went back to the newsroom.

The papers had just come up from the pressroom and there on the front page was my story with a twelve-point by-line and the headline spread across eight columns.

Also on the front page was a picture of Joy holding a skunk and seeming charmed about it. Underneath the picture was the story she had written, and one of the jokers on the copydesk had achieved one of the standard sappy headlines on it.

I went over to the city desk and stood alongside Gavin. "Any luck," I asked him, "in your hunt for Bennett?"

"No luck at all," he told me wrathfully. "I don't think there was ever such a man. I think you made him up."

"Maybe Bruce—"

"I called Bruce. Bruce says he figured Bennett was staying at one of the hotels. Said the man never talked anything but business. Never once mentioned personalities."

"The hotels?"

"No, and he never has been. None of them has had a Bennett for the last three weeks. We're working on the motels now, but I tell you, Parker, it's a waste of time. There isn't such a man."

"Maybe he's registered under a different name. Check on bald men . . ."

"That's a hot one," snarled Gavin. "Have you any idea how many bald men register in our hotels each day?"

"No," I said, "I haven't."

Gavin was in his usual home-edition lather, and there wasn't any use in talking further with him. I walked away and started across the room to have a word with Dow. But I saw he wasn't there, so I stopped off at my desk.

I picked up the paper that was lying there and sat down to look at it. I read through my story and was furious with myself over a couple of paragraphs that read jumbled up and jerky. It always happens that way when you write a story under pressure. You get it down the best way that you can and then, for the next edition, you get it all smoothed out.

So I jerked the typewriter over to the desk and rewrote the paragraphs. I used a straightedge to tear the printed story from the page and pasted it up on two sheets of copy paper. I crossed out the two offending paragraphs and marked them for a sub. I went through the story again and caught a couple of typos and fixed up another place or two to make the language better.

It was a wonder, I told myself, that I'd got the story down at all with the copydesk leaning back and hollering that it was way past deadline and Gavin there beside me, jigging from one foot to the other and panting out each line.

I took the inserts and the marked-up copy over to the city desk and dropped them in the basket. Then I went back to my desk again and picked up the mangled paper. I read Joy's story, and it was a lulu. Then I looked for the story Dow had gone out to the airport to get and it wasn't in the paper. I looked around again and Dow wasn't anywhere in sight.

I dropped the paper on the desk top and sat there, doing nothing, idly remembering what had happened in Franklin's conference room that morning. But all I could remember was the fly crawling on the skull.

Then, suddenly, there was something else.

Gunderson had asked me if there had been anything about Bennett that might be a clue to his identity and I had said there wasn't.

But I had told him wrong. For there had been something. Not a clue exactly, but something damned peculiar. I remembered now—it was the smell of him. Shaving lotion, I had thought when I first got a whiff of it. But not any kind of lotion I had ever smelled before. Not the kind of lotion any other man would ever tolerate. Not that it was loud or strong—for there had been no more than that correct, faint suggestion of it. But it had been the kind of odor one does not associate with a human being.

I sat there and tried to classify it, tried to think of something with which I might compare it. But I couldn't, because, for the life of me, I couldn't remember exactly what it had smelled like. But I was mortally certain I would recognize it if I ever came in contact with it again.

I got up and walked over to Joy's desk. She stopped typing as I came up to her. She lifted her head to look at me, and her eyes were bright and shiny, as if she had been trying to keep herself from crying.

"What's the matter here?" I asked.

"Parker," she said. "Those poor people! It's enough to break one's heart."

"What poor—" I started to say, and then I had a hunch what had happened to her.

"How did you get hold of that one?" I demanded.

"Dow wasn't here," she said. "They came in asking for him. And everyone else was busy. So Gavin brought them over."

"I was going to do it," I told her. "Dow told me about it and I said I would. Then this Franklin's thing came up and I forgot everything about it. There was supposed to be just a man. You said them . . ."

"He brought his wife and children and they sat down and looked at me with those big, solemn eyes of theirs. They told me how they had sold their home because it wasn't big enough for a growing family and now they can't find another one. They have to be out of their house in another day or two and they have nowhere at all to go. They sit there and tell their troubles to you and they look so hopeful at you. As if you were Santa Claus or the Good Fairy or something of the sort. As if your pencil were a wand. As if they were confident you can solve their problems and make everything all right. People have such funny ideas about newspapers, Parker. They think we practice magic. They think if they can get their stories into print, something good will happen. They think that we are people who can make miracles. And you sit there and look back at them, and you know you can't."

"I know," I told her. "Just don't let it get you. You mustn't be a bleeder. You've got to harden up."

"Parker," she said, "get out of here and let me finish this. Gavin has been yelling for it for the last ten minutes."

She wasn't kidding me a second. She wanted me out of there so she could burst out crying quietly.

"OK," I said. "Be seeing you tonight."

Back at my desk, I put away the columns I had written earlier in the morning. Then I got my hat and coat and went out to have a drink.

7

Ed was alone in his place, standing behind the bar with his elbows on it and his hands holding up his face. He didn't look so good.

I got up on a stool and laid five dollars down.

"Give me a quick one, Ed," I said. "I really need it bad."

"Keep your money in your pocket," he told me gruffly. "The drinks are all on me."

I almost fell off the stool. He'd never done a thing like that before.

"You out of your mind?" I asked him.

"Not that at all," said Ed, reaching for my brand of Scotch. "I'm going out of business. I'm setting them up for my old, loyal customers whenever they come in."

"Made your pile," I said carelessly, for the guy is always joking, anything at all just to get a yak.

"I've lost my lease," he told me.

I sympathized with him. "Well, that's too bad," I said. "But there must be a dozen places you can get, right here in the neighborhood."

Ed shook his head dolefully. "I'm closed up," he said. "I have no place to go. I've checked everywhere. If you want to know what I think, Parker, it's dirty pool down at the city hall. Someone wants my license. Someone slipped a couple of aldermen a little extra dough."

He poured the drink and shoved it over to me.

He poured one for himself, and that is something that no bartender ever does. It wasn't hard to see that Ed just didn't give a damn.

"Twenty-eight years," he told me mournfully. "That's how long I've been here. I always run a respectable joint. You know, Parker, that I did. You've been a regular customer. You've seen how I run the place. You never saw no rowdy stuff and you never saw no women. And you seen the cops in here, plenty of times, lined up and drinking on the house."

I agreed with him. Everything he'd said was the gospel truth. "I know that, Ed," I said. "Christ, I don't see how that gang of ours will get the paper out if you have to close. The boys won't have a place to go to get the taste out of their mouths. There isn't another bar within eight blocks of the office."

"I don't know what I'll do," he said. "I'm too young to quit and I haven't got the money. I have to earn a living. I could work for someone else, of course. Almost anyone in town would find a place for me. But I've always owned my own joint and it would take some getting used to. I don't mind telling you it would come a little hard."

"It's a stinking shame," I said.

"Me and Franklin's," he said. "We'll go out together. I just read it in the paper. The story that you wrote. The town won't be the same without Franklin's."

I told him the town wouldn't be the same without him, either, and he poured me another drink, but this time he didn't take one for himself.

He stood there and I sat there and we talked it over—about Franklin's closing and the lease he'd lost and neither of us knowing what the goddamn world might be coming to. He set up a couple more and had another one himself and we had some more after that and I made him let me pay for them. I told him even if he was going out of business he couldn't just give away his liquor and he said he'd made enough off me in the last six or seven years that he could afford an afternoon of some free ones.

Some customers came in and Ed went to take care of them. Since they were strangers, or maybe just poor customers, he let them pay him for their drinks. He rang up the tab on the register and gave them their change and then came back to me. So we talked the situation over once again, repeating ourselves a good deal without noticing or caring.

It was two o'clock before I got out of there.

I promised Ed, somewhat sentimentally, that I'd come back for one last talk before he closed up the place.

I should have been drunk, the amount of liquor I'd poured into me. But I wasn't drunk. I was just depressed.

I started back to the office, but halfway there I decided that it wasn't worth it. I had only an hour or so to go to fill out the day, and this late in the afternoon, with most of the editions put to bed, there'd be nothing I could do. Except maybe write some columns, and I didn't feel like writing any columns. So I decided I'd go home. I'd work over the weekend, getting out the columns, to make up for goofing off.

So I went to the parking lot and got my car untangled and headed home, driving slow and carefully so no cop would pick me up.

8

I pulled into the alley and swung into the area back of the apartment building, parking the car in the stall that was reserved for it.

It was peaceful back there and I sat for a while in the car before getting out. The sun was warm and the building, wrapped around three sides of the area, kept out any wind. A scrubby poplar tree grew in one angle of the building, and the sun was full upon it, so that, with its autumn-colored leaves, it glowed like a tree of promise. The air was drowsy, filled with sun and time, and I could hear the clicking toenails of a dog trotting up the alley. The dog came in sight and saw me. He sat down and cocked anxious ears at me. He was half the size of a horse and he was so shaggy he was shapeless. He lifted a ponderous hind leg and solemnly scratched a flea.

"Hi, pup," I said.

He got up and trotted down the alley. Just before he went out of sight, he stopped for a second and looked back at me.

I got out of the car and went down the alley and around the corner to the building's entrance. The lobby was hushed and empty and my footsteps echoed in it. There were a couple of letters in my mailbox and I jammed them in my pocket, then trudged slowly up the stairs to the second floor.

First of all, I told myself, I would have a nap. Getting up as early as I had was catching up with me.

The semicircle of carpeting still was missing from before my door and I stopped and stared at it. I'd almost forgotten it, but now last night's incident came back with a rush. I shivered looking at it, fumbling in my pocket for the keys so I could get inside and shut the semicircle in the hall behind me.

Inside the apartment, I shut the door behind me and tossed my hat and coat into a chair and stood there and looked around me. And it was all right. There was nothing wrong with it. There was nothing stirring in it. There was nothing strange.

It wasn't a fancy place, but I was satisfied with it. It was my very own and it was the first place for a long time that I'd lived in long enough to really count as home. I had been there six years and I fitted into it. I had my gun cabinet against one wall and the hi-fi in the corner, and one entire end of the front room was filled with books, piled into a monstrous bookcase I'd cobbled up myself.

I went into the kitchen and looked in the refrigerator and found tomato juice. I poured a glass of it and sat down at the table and, as I did, the letters in my pocket rustled, so I pulled them out. One was from the Guild, and I knew it was another warning about delinquent dues. The second was from some firm with a many-jointed name.

I opened that one up and pulled out a single sheet.

I read: *Dear Mr. Graves: This is to notify you that under the provisions of clause 31 we are terminating your lease on apartment 210, Wellington Arms, effective January 1.*

There was a signature at the bottom of it that I was unable to make out.

And there was something terribly fishy about it, for these people who had sent the letter didn't own the building. Old George owned it—Old George Weber, who lived down on the first floor in apartment 116.

I started to get up, intending to go charging down the stairs and ask Old George just what the hell this meant. Then I remembered that Old George and Mrs. George were out in California.

Maybe, I told myself, Old George had turned the operation of the building over to these people for the time that he was gone. And if that were the case, there was some mistake. Old George and I were pals. He'd never throw me out. He sneaked up to my place to have a drink or two every now and then, and every Tuesday evening the two of us played pinochle, and almost every fall he went out to South Dakota with me for some pheasant shooting.

I took another look at the letterhead and saw that the name of the firm was Ross, Martin, Park & Gobel. In little letters under the firm name was another line, which said "Property Management."

I wondered exactly what clause 31 might be. I thought of looking it up, then realized that I had no idea where I'd put the copy of my lease. It was probably in the apartment somewhere, but I had not the least idea.

I went into the living room and dialed the number of Ross, Martin, Park & Gobel.

A telephone voice answered—a professionally trained, high-pitched, feminine, how-happy-that-you-called voice.

"Miss," I told her, "someone at your office has pulled a boner. I have a letter here throwing me out of my apartment."

There was a click and a man came on. I told him what had happened.

"How come your firm is mixed up in this?" I asked him. "The owner, to my knowledge, is my good neighbor and old friend, George Weber."

"You are wrong there, Mr. Graves," this gent told me in a voice that for calmness and pomposity would have done credit to a judge. "Mr. Weber sold the property in question to a client of ours several weeks ago."

"Old George never told me a word about it."

"Maybe he simply overlooked it," said the man at the other end, and his voice held a tone just short of a sneer. "Maybe he didn't get around to it; Our client took possession the middle of the month."

"And immediately sent out a notice canceling my lease?"

"All the leases, Mr. Graves. He needs the property for other purposes."

"Like a parking lot, for instance."

"That's right," said the man. "Like a parking lot."

I hung up. I didn't even bother to say good-bye to him. I knew I wouldn't get anywhere talking to that joker.

I sat quietly in the living room and listened to the sound of traffic on the street outside. A couple of chattering girls went walking past, giggling as they talked. The sun shone through the westward-facing windows and the light was warm and mellow.

But there was a coldness in the room—a terrible iciness that crept from some far dimension and seeped not into the room but into my very bones.

First it had been Franklin's, then it was Ed's bar, and now it was this place that I called my home. No, that was wrong, I thought: first it had been the man who had phoned Dow and who had finally talked with Joy, telling her how he had been unable to find a house to buy. He and all those others who were being quietly desperate in the classified columns—they had been the first.

I picked up the paper from the desk where I had thrown it when I came into the room and folded it back to the want ads and there they were, just as Dow had told me. Column after column of them under the headings of "Houses Wanted" or "Apts. Wanted." Little pitiful lines of type crying out for shelter.

What was going on? I wondered. What had happened so suddenly to all the living space? Where were all the new apartments that had sprouted, the acre after acre of suburban building?

I dropped the paper on the floor and dialed a realtor I knew. A secretary answered and I had to hold the line until he finished with another call.

Finally he came on.

"Parker," he asked, "what can I do for you?"

"I'm being thrown out," I said. "I need a roof above my head."

"Oh my God!" he said.

"A room will do," I told him. "Just one big room if that's the best there is."

"Look, Parker, how long have you got?"

"Until the first of the year."

"Maybe in that time I can do something for you. The situation may ease up a bit. I'll keep you in mind. Almost anything, you say?"

"Is it really that bad, Bob?"

"I got them in the office. I got them on the phone. People hunting homes."

"But what happened? There are all those new apartment houses and the big developments. They had signs out front, advertised for rent or sale all summer."

"I don't know," he said, and he sounded frantic. "I wouldn't even try to answer. I just can't understand it. I could sell a thousand homes. I could rent any number of apartments. But I haven't got a one. I'm sitting here, going stony broke, because I have no listings. They all ran down to zero a good ten days ago. I have people pleading with me. They offer bribes to me. They think I'm holding out. I have more customers than I ever had before and there's no way I can do business with them."

"New people coming into town?"

"God, I don't think so, Parker. Not this many of them."

"New couples starting out?"

"I tell you, honest, half of the folks waiting for me are older people who sold their homes because the families had grown up and they didn't need a big house any more. And a lot of the others are people who sold their places because their families were increasing and they needed room."

"And now," I said, "there is no room at all."

"That's the size of it," he said.

There was nothing more to say.

I said it.

"Thanks, Bob."

"I'll keep watch for you," he said. He didn't sound too hopeful.

I hung up and sat there and wondered what was going on. There was something going on—I was sure of that. This was not just a situation brought about by an abnormal demand. Here was something that defied all rules of economics. There was a story somewhere; I could almost smell it. Franklin's had been sold and Ed had lost his lease and Old George had sold this building and people were storming realty offices in a mad attempt to find a place to live.

I got up and put on my hat and coat. I tried not to notice the semicircle out of the carpeting when I went out the door.

I had a terrible hunch—a terrifying hunch.

The apartment building stood on the edge of a neighborhood shopping area, one that had developed years before, long before anyone had thought of sticking shopping centers helter-skelter way out in the sticks.

If my hunch was right, the answer might lie in the shopping area—in any shopping area.

I set out, hunting for that answer.

9

Ninety minutes later I had my answer and I was scared stone cold.

Most of the business houses in the area had lost their leases or were about to lose them. Several with long leases had sold their businesses. Most of the buildings apparently had changed hands within the last few weeks.

I talked with men who were desperate and others who had become resigned. And a few who were angry and another few who admitted they were licked.

"I tell you," one druggist said, "maybe it is just as well. With the tax structure as it stands and all the regulations and the governmental interference, I sometimes wonder just how smart it is to remain in business. Sure, I looked for another location. But that was pure reflex. Habit dies hard in almost any man. But there's no location. There's nowhere for me to go. So I'll just sell out my stock as best I can and get this monkey off my back, then wait and see what happens."

"Any plans?" I asked.

"Well, the wife and I have been talking for some time about a long vacation. But we never took it. Never got around to taking it. This business tied me down and it's hard to get good help."

And there was the barber who had waved his scissors and snipped them angrily.

"Christ," he said, "a man can't make a living any longer. They won't let you."

I wanted to ask him who *they* were, but he didn't give me a chance to get in a single word.

"God knows I make a poor enough living as it is," he said. "Barbering isn't what it used to be. Haircuts are all you get. Now and then a shampoo, but that is all. We used to shave them and give them facials and all of them wanted stickum on their hair. But now all we get is haircuts. And now they won't even let me keep the little that I have."

I managed to ask who *they* were, and he couldn't tell me. He was angry that I asked. He thought I was smarting off.

Two old family establishments (among others), each of which owned its building, had held out against the offers which had been made them, each more attractive than the last.

"You know Mr. Graves," said an old gentleman at one of the hold-out business houses, "there might have been a time when I would have taken one of the offers. I suppose that I am foolish that I didn't. But I'm too old a man. Me and this store have become so entangled we're a part of one another. To sell out the business would be like selling out myself. I don't suppose that you can understand that."

"I think I do," I said.

He put up a pale old hand, with the startling blue of veins standing out against the porcelain of his skin, and smoothed the thin white thatch of hair that clung plastered to his skull.

"There's such a thing as pride," he told me. "Pride in a way of doing business. No one else, I can assure you, would carry on this business in the same manner that I do. There are no manners in the world today, young man. There isn't any kindness. And no consideration. There's no such thing as thinking the best of one's fellowmen. The business world has become a bookkeeping operation, performed by machines and by men who are very like machines in that they have no soul. There is no honor and no trust and the ethics have become the ethics of a wolf pack."

He reached out the porcelain hand and laid it on my arm so lightly I couldn't feel its touch.

"You say all my neighbors have lost their leases or sold out?"

"The most of them."

"Jake up the street—he hasn't? The one in the furniture business. He's a thieving old scoundrel, but he thinks the same as I."

I told him he was right. Jake wasn't selling out, one of the half dozen or so who hadn't.

"He's the same as me," the old man said. "We look on business as a trust and privilege. These others only see it as a way of making money. Jake has his sons he can leave the business to, and that may make a difference. Maybe that's another reason he is hanging on. It is different with me. I have no family. There is just my sister. Just the two of us. When we are gone, the business will go with us. But so long as we live, we stay here, serving the public as honorably as we can. For I tell you, sir, that business is more than just a counting of the profits. It is a chance for service, a chance to make a contribution. It is the glue that keeps our civilization stuck together, and there can be no prouder profession for any man to follow."

It sounded like a muted trumpet call from some other era, and that, perhaps, was exactly what it was. For a moment I sensed the thrill of proud-bright banners waving in the blue and I felt the newness and the clearness that was gone forever now.

And the old man may have seen the same thing that I had seen, for he said: "It is all tarnished now. Only here and there, in a few secluded corners, can we keep it shining bright."

"Thank you, sir," I said. "You've done me a lot of good."

As we shook hands in parting, I wondered why I should have told him that. Wondering why, I knew it was the truth—that somehow he'd done something, or said something, to put back some faith in me. Faith in what? I wondered, and I wasn't sure. Faith in Man, perhaps. Faith in the world. Perhaps, even, some faith in myself.

I went out of the store and stood on the sidewalk and shivered, cold in the last warmness of the day.

For now it was not just happenstance, whatever it might be that was going on. It wasn't only Franklin's or the apartment in which I lived. It wasn't only Ed who had lost his lease. It wasn't only people who could find no place to live.

There was a pattern here—a pattern and a vicious purpose. And a thoroughness and a method that were diabolic.

And somewhere behind it all, a smooth-working organization that moved with secrecy and speed. For apparently all the transactions had been concluded within the last few months and all of them aimed at a roughly coincidental closing date.

One thing I didn't know, and could only guess at, was whether one man or a small group of men or a vast army of them had been needed to do the dickering, to make the offers, to finally close the deals. I had tried to find out, but no one seemed to know. Most of the men I had talked with were those who had leased their quarters and had no way of knowing.

I walked to a corner and went into a drugstore. I squeezed into a phone booth and dialed the office. When a phone gal answered, I asked to speak with Dow.

"Where you been?" he asked.

"Goofing off," I told him.

"We've been going wild up here," Dow said. "Hennessey's announced they had lost their lease."

"Hennessey's!" Although I don't know why I should have been surprised, knowing what I knew.

"It isn't possible," said Dow. "Not the two of them in a single day."

Hennessey's was the second loop department store. With both it and Franklin's gone, the downtown shopping district would become a desert.

"You missed the first edition with your airport interview," I told him, stalling for time, wondering how much I ought to tell him.

"The plane was late," he said.

"How did they keep it so quiet?" I demanded. "There wasn't a single rumor about the Franklin's deal."

"I went over to see Bruce," said Dow. "I asked him that. He showed me the contract—not for publication, just between the two of us. There was a clause in there which automatically canceled out the sale in case of premature announcement."

"And Hennessey's?"

"First National owned the building. They probably had the same clause in their contract. Hennessey's can stay on for another year, but there's no other building—"

"The price would have to be good. At least good enough for them not to want to lose the sale. To keep that quiet, I mean."

"In the Franklin's case, it was. Again, not for publication, in strictest confidence, it was twice as much as anyone in their right mind would pay. And after paying that much, the new owner shuts it down. That's what hurts Bruce the worst. As if someone hated Franklin's so much they'd pay twice what it was worth just to shut it down."

Dow hesitated for a moment; then he said: "Parker, it makes no sense at all. No business sense, that is."

And I was thinking: That explained all the secrecy. Why there had been no rumors. Why Old George had failed to tell me he had sold the building—scurrying off to California so his friends and tenants couldn't ask him why he hadn't told them he had sold the building.

I stood there in the booth, wondering if it could be possible that there had been restrictive clauses in each one of the contracts and if the dates of those restrictive clauses could have been the same.

It seemed incredible, of course, but the whole thing was incredible.

"Parker," asked Dow, "are you still there?"

"Yes," I said. "Yes, I'm still here. Tell me one thing, Dow. Who was it that bought Franklin's?"

"I don't know," he said. "Some property management outfit called Ross, Martin, Park & Gobel had some hand in drawing up the papers. I called them—"

"And they told you they were handling it for a client. They were not at liberty to tell you who the client was."

"Exactly. How did you know that?"

"Just a guess," I said. "This whole thing stinks to heaven."

"I checked up on Ross, Martin, Park & Gobel," said Dow. "They have been in business a sum total of ten weeks."

I said a silly thing. "Ed lost his lease today. It is going to be lonesome."

"Ed?"

"Yeah. Ed's bar."

"Parker, what is going on?"

"Darned if I know," I said. "So what else is new?"

"Money. I checked. The banks are overflowing with money. Cash money. They've been busy for the last week scooping it in. People come in loaded and are socking it away."

"Well, well," I said, "it is nice to know the area's economy is in such good condition."

"Parker," snapped Dow, "what in hell is the matter with you?"

"Not a thing," I said. "See you in the morning."

I hung up quick, before he could ask me any more.

I stood there and wondered why I hadn't told him what I knew. There was no reason why I shouldn't have. There was, in fact, probably every reason that I should have, for it fell in line of duty.

And yet I hadn't done it, because I had been unable to, couldn't bring myself to do it. Almost as if by not saying it, I'd keep it from being true. Almost as if I didn't say it, there'd be no truth in it.

And that, of course, was silly.

I got out of the booth and went down the street. I stood on the corner and dug into my pocket and brought out the notice I had gotten in the mail. Ross, Martin, Park & Gobel was located in the loop—in the old McCandless Building, one of those ancient brownstone tombs that were marked for early razing by the city's redevelopment authority.

I could see the setup—the creaking elevators and the stairs with marble treads and with great bronze railings, blackened now with age; the solemn corridors with their wainscoting of oak so old it shone with the polish of its aging, with the ceilings high and the doors with great squares of frosted glass reaching halfway down them. And on the first floor the arcade with the stamp shop and the tobacco shop, with the magazine counter and the shoe-shine corner and a dozen other little businesses.

I looked at my watch and it was after five o'clock. The street was packed with a solid stream of cars, the beginning of the homeward rush, with the traffic streaming westward, heading for one of the two great highways that led out into the area of huge housing developments and cozy little neighborhoods tucked away among the lakes and hills.

The sun had set and it was that moment when daylight is beginning to fade and twilight has not quite yet set in. The nicest part of the day, I thought, for people who weren't troubled or had nothing on their minds.

I walked slowly down the street, turning over slowly what was frying in my brain. I didn't like it much, but it was a hunch, and I'd learned from long experience not to turn my back on hunches. Too many had paid off in the past to allow me to ignore them.

I found a hardware store and went into it. I bought a glass cutter, feeling guilty as I did it. I put it in my pocket and went out on the street again.

There were more people on the sidewalk now and more cars honking in the street. I stood well up against a building and watched the crowd flow past.

Perhaps, I told myself, I should drop it now. Perhaps the smart thing to do was simply to go home and then in an hour or so get dressed and go and pick up Joy.

I stood there undecided and I almost dropped it, but there was something in me nagging, something that would not let me drop it.

A cab came down the street, hemmed in by the cars. It stopped with the stream of traffic, caught by a changing traffic light, almost in front of me. I saw that it was empty and I didn't stop to think. I didn't give myself a chance to make a real decision. I stepped out to the curb and the cabby saw me and swung the door open so I could get in.

"Where to, mister?"

I gave him the intersection just beyond the McCandless Building.

The light changed and the cab edged along.

"Have you noticed, mister," said the cabby, by way of starting a conversation, "how the world has gone to hell?"

10

The McCandless Building was just the way I had imagined it, the way all the old brownstone office buildings were.

The third-floor corridor was hushed, with the faint light of the dying day filtering into the windows at its end. The carpet was worn and the walls were stained; the woodwork, for all its ancient shine, had a tired and beaten look.

The office doors were frosted glass, with the peeling, tattered gold of firm names fixed upon them. Each door, I noted, was fitted with a lock independent of the ancient lock built into the knob assembly.

I paced the length of the hall to be sure there was no one around. All the offices apparently were deserted. This was a Friday night and the office workers would have gotten out as soon as possible to begin their weekend. It was too early yet for the cleaning women to come in.

The office of Ross, Martin, Park & Gobel was near the end of the corridor. I tried the door and it was locked, as I knew it would be. I took out the glass cutter and settled down to work. It was not an easy job. When you cut a piece of glass, you're supposed to lay it on a flat surface and work at it from above. That way you can manage, if you're careful, to get a sure and steady pressure so that the little wheel can score the glass. And here I was, trying to cut a piece of glass that was standing on its edge.

It took me quite a while, but I finally got the glass scored and put the cutter back into my pocket. I stood for a moment, listening, making sure there was no one in the corridor or coming up the stairs. Then I bumped the glass with my elbow and the scored piece cracked and broke, leaning at an angle, still held within the doorframe. I nudged it again and it broke and fell inside the room. And I had a fist-size hole just above the lock.

Being careful not to come in contact with the jagged bits of broken glass still held within the frame, I put in my hand and found the knob that turned the lock. I twisted and the lock came back. With my other hand, I turned the outside knob and pushed and the door came open.

I oozed into the place and shut the door behind me, then slid along the wall and stood there for a long moment, with my back against the wall.

I felt the hairs rising on the back of my neck and my heart was thumping, for the smell was there—the smell of Bennett's shaving lotion. Just the faint suggestion of a smell, but unmistakable, as if the man had put it on that morning and in the afternoon had brushed past me on the street. I tried once again to define it, but there was nothing I could compare it with. It was the kind of odor I had never smelled in all my life. Nothing wrong with it—not very wrong, that is—but a kind of smell I had never known before.

Out in the space beyond where I stood against the wall were dark shapes and humps, and as I stared at them and as my eyes became accustomed to the darkness of the place I could see that it was just an office and not a thing unusual. The dark shapes and black humps were desks and filing cabinets and all the other furniture you expect to find inside a business office.

I stood tensed and waiting, but absolutely nothing happened. The grayness of deep twilight seeped in through the windows, but it seemed to stop just beyond the windows; it did not penetrate into the room. And the place was quiet, so utterly quiet that it was unnerving.

I looked around the room and now, for the first time, I noticed something strange. In one corner of the room an alcove was curtained off—a strange arrangement, certainly, for a business office.

I looked around the rest of the office, forcing my eyes to go over it almost inch by inch, alert to the slightest thing out of the ordinary. But there was nothing else—nothing strange at all except the curtained alcove. And the lotion smell.

Cautiously, I moved out from the wall and across the room. I didn't know exactly what I was afraid of, but there was a fear of some sort crouching in the room.

I halted at the desk in front of the alcove and snapped on a desk lamp. I knew it wasn't smart. I had broken into this office, and now I was advertising it by turning on the light. But I took the chance. I wanted to see, immediately and without question, what was back of the drapes closing off the alcove.

In the light I could see that the drapes were of some heavy, dark material and that they were hung on a traverse rod. Moving to one side and groping, I found the cords. I pulled and the drapes parted, folding smoothly out to either side. Behind the drapes was a row of garments, all neatly ranged on hangers which were hung upon a pole.

I stood there, gaping at them. And as I looked at them I began to see them, not as a mass of garments, but as separate garments. There were men's suits and topcoats; there were half a dozen shirts; there was a hanger full of ties. On the shelf above the rack, hats were primly ranged. There were women's suits and dresses and some rather frilly garments that I suppose you would call gowns. There was underclothing, both men's and women's; there were socks and stockings. Underneath the clothing, on a long rack standing on the floor, shoes were precisely placed, again both men's and women's.

And this was stark crazy. A place to hang topcoats, raincoats, jackets, a place to put the hats—if there were no closet, it would be very likely that some fussbudget in the office might fix up a place like this. But here were complete wardrobes for everyone in the entire office, from the boss down to the lowliest of the secretaries.

I racked my brains for an explanation, but there wasn't any.

And the craziest thing about it was that the office now was empty, that everyone had gone—and they had left their clothes behind. Certainly they would not have left the office without wearing any clothes.

I moved slowly along the line of clothing, putting out my hand to touch them, to make sure they were really fabric, that they were really there. They were ordinary fabrics. And they were really there.

As I walked along the line, I felt a sudden draft of coldness at the level of my ankles. Someone had left a window open—that was the way it felt. As I took another step, the draft as suddenly was gone.

I made my way to the end of the rack of clothing, turned around, and walked back again. Once again the coldness hit my ankles.

There was something wrong here. There was no window open. For a draft from an open window does not creep along the floor at ankle height; nor is it channeled so that with one step you are in it and the next step out.

There was something behind the rack of clothes. And what, in the name of God, could be cold behind a rack of clothes?

Unthinking, I hunkered down and swept the clothes apart and found where the coldness came from.

It came from a hole, a hole that went through the McCandless Building, but not outside the building, not clear through the building, for if it had been a simple hole knocked clear through the wall, I would have seen the lights on the street outside.

There were no lights. There was an utter darkness and a giddiness and a cold that was more than simple cold—more like the complete lack of any heat at all. Here, I sensed—and I don't know how I sensed it—was a lack of something, perhaps the lack of everything, a complete negation of the form and light and heat that was upon the Earth. I sensed a motion, although I could see no motion—a sort of eddying of the darkness and the cold, as if the two were being stirred by some mysterious mixer, a sucking whirlpool of the darkness and the cold. As I stared into the hole, the giddiness that was in it tried to tip me forward and to suck me in and I jerked back in terror, sprawling on the floor.

I lay there, stiff and tense with fright, and felt the seeping cold and watched the motion of the clothing as it fell back in place to mask the hole punched in the wall.

Slowly I got to my feet and edged toward the desk, putting the barrier of the desk between myself and what I'd found behind the curtain.

And what was it I had found?

The question hammered at me and there was no answer, as there was no answer to the clothing hanging in a row.

I put out a hand to grab the desk, seeking something solid to which I might anchor against this unknown menace. But instead of the desk, my fingers grasped a basket and tipped it so that the papers in it fell onto the floor. I got down on hands and knees and scrabbled for the papers, stacking them together. They were all neatly folded and they had a *legal* feel, that funny, important texture that legal papers have.

I got off my knees and dumped them on the desk top and ran quickly through them, and every one of them—every single one— was a property transfer. And every one of them was made out to a Fletcher Atwood.

The name rang a distant bell and I stood there groping, fumbling back through a cluttered—and a faulty—memory for some clue that would let me peg the man.

Somewhere in the past the name of Fletcher Atwood had meant something to me. Somewhere I'd met the man, or written about him, or talked to him on the telephone. He was a name filed away deep inside the brain, but so long forgotten, perhaps even at the time of so little moment, that the fact and place and time had slipped clean away from me.

It was something that Joy had said to me, it seemed. Walking past my desk and stopping to say a word or two—the little idle talk of a busy newsroom where no name may live for long in the headlong rush of hourly happenings.

Something about a house, it seemed—a house that Atwood had bought.

And just like that I had it. Fletcher Atwood was the man who'd bought the storied Belmont place out on Timber Lane. A man of mystery who had never fitted in with the horsey set in that exclusive area. Who had never, actually, lived in the house he'd bought; who might spend a night or week there but had never really lived there; who had no family and no friends; who, furthermore, seemed to have no wish for friends.

Timber Lane had resented him at first, for the Belmont place at one time had been the center of that elusive thing which Timber Lane had called society. He was never mentioned now—not in Timber Lane. He was a moldy skeleton that had been shoved aside into a dusty cupboard.

And was this revenge? I wondered, spreading out the transfers underneath the lamp. Although it scarcely could be that, for there'd been no evidence, one way or the other, that Atwood had ever cared what Timber Lane might have thought of him.

Here were properties that ran into billions. Here were proud business firms, hoary with tradition and gemmed with family names; here small industries; here the ancient buildings that had been a byword in the town as long as the oldest man remembered. All of them transferred to Fletcher Atwood in ponderous, precise legal language—all stacked here and waiting to be processed and filed.

Waiting here, perhaps, I speculated, because no one as yet had had the time to file them. Waiting because there was too much other work to do. Too much, I wondered, of what kind of other work?

It seemed incredible, but here it was—the very legal proof that one man had bought up, in a bundle as it were, a more than respectable segment of the city's business district.

No man could have the amount of money that was represented in this batch of papers. Nor, perhaps, any group of men. But if, indeed, some men had, what could be their purpose?

To buy up a city?

For this was but one small group of papers, left lying in a naked basket atop the desk as if the papers were of small importance. In this very office there were undoubtedly many times their number. And if Fletcher Atwood, or the men he represented, had bought out this city, what did he mean to do with it?

I put the papers back into the basket and moved out from the desk back to the rack of clothes. I stared up at the shelf where the hats were ranged in line and I saw, among the hats, what seemed to be a shoe box.

Perhaps a box with more papers in it?

I stood on tiptoe and worked the box out with my fingertips until it tipped and I could get a grip on it. It was heavier than I had expected. I carried it back to the desk and placed it underneath the lamp and took the cover off.

The box was filled with dolls—and yet something more than dolls, without the studied artificiality one associates with dolls. Here were dolls so human that one wondered if they might not be actual humans, shrunken down to something like four inches long but shrunken in such an expert manner that their proportions were unchanged.

And lying on top of that mass of dolls was a doll that was the perfect image of that Bennett who had sat with Bruce Montgomery at the conference table!

11

I stood there thunderstruck, staring at the doll. And the more I looked at it, the more it looked like Bennett, a stark-naked Bennett, a little Bennett doll that waited for someone to dress him and sit him in a chair behind a conference table. He was so realistic that I could imagine the fly crawling on his skull.

Slowly, almost afraid to touch the doll—afraid that when I touched it, it might turn out to be alive—I reached down into the shoe box and lifted Bennett out. He was heavier than I had expected, heavier than any normal, four-inch doll should be. I held him underneath the light, and there was no question that this thing I held between my fingers was an exact replica of the living man. The eyes were cold and stony and the lips as thin and straight. The skull looked not simply bald but sterile, as if it had never grown a hair. The body was the kind of body that a man near the end of middle age would have—a body tending toward flabbiness, but with the flabbiness held in check by planned exercise and a close attention to very careful living.

I laid Bennett on the desk and reached into the box again, and this time I picked up a girl doll—a very lovely blonde. I held her underneath the lamp, and there was no doubt of it: here was no doll as such, but the faithful model of a woman with no detail of anatomy ignored. She was so close to living that it seemed one would only have to speak a certain magic word to bring her back to life. Delicate and dainty and lovely to the fingertips, she had about her none of the mechanical irregularities or grotesqueness of a manufactured article.

I laid her down alongside Bennett and put my hand into the box and stirred the dolls around. There were a lot of them, perhaps twenty or thirty, and there were many types. There were alert young eager beavers and old staid business beagles and the slick, smooth maleness of the accomplished operator; there were the prim career girls, the querulous old maids, the young things in the office.

I quit stirring them around and went back to the blonde again. I was fascinated by her.

I picked her up and had another look at her and tried to be professional about it by puzzling at the material with which the doll was made. It might have been a plastic, although, if so, a type I'd never seen before. It was hard and heavy yet had a yielding quality. If you squeezed hard enough, it dented and then sprang back again when the pressure was released. And it had the faintest feel of a certain warmth. The funny thing about it was that it seemed to have no texture, or so fine a texture it could not be detected.

I rummaged through the box again, picking up the dolls, and they were all the same in the skill and artistry of their manufacture.

I put Bennett and the blonde back with the rest of them and put the box back on the shelf, carefully inserting it into the space between the hats.

I backed away and looked around the office and there was a roaring in my brain at the madness of it—the dolls upon the shelf and the clothes upon the rack, the hole with the giddiness of cold and the stack of papers that bought out half a city.

Reaching out my hand, I closed the drapes. They slid easily into place with the faintest rustle, closing in the dolls and the clothes and the hole, but not closing in the madness, for the madness still was there. You could almost feel it, as if it were a shadow moving in the darkness outside the circle of the lamplight.

Whatever does one do, I asked myself, when he stumbles into something that is impossible of belief and yet with its surface facts entirely evident? For they were evident; one thing one might have imagined or misinterpreted, but there was no possibility of imagining all the things within this office.

I turned out the lamp and the darkness closed in, muffling the room. With my hand still on the lamp switch, I stood unmoving, listening, but there was no sound.

Tiptoeing, I made my way among the desks back to the door, and every step I took I sensed the creeping danger at my back— an imagined danger, but strong and terrifying. Perhaps it was the thought that there had to be a danger and a threat, that the things I had uncovered were not meant to be uncovered, that there must, in all logic, be a certain built-in protection for them.

I went out into the corridor, closed the door behind me, and stood a moment with my back against the wall. The corridor itself was dark. Lights had been turned on in the stairwell and faint light, reflected from the street below, filtered through the window.

There was nothing stirring, no sign of life at all. The squeal of braking wheels, the honking of a car horn, the gay laughter of a girl came up faintly from the street.

And now, for some reason I could not understand, it became important that I should leave the building without being seen. As if it were a game, a most important game with very much at stake, and I could not risk the ending of it by being apprehended.

I went cat-footing down the corridor and had nearly reached the stairs when I felt the rush.

Felt is not the word, perhaps, nor is sensed. For it was not sensing; it was knowing. There was no sound, no movement, no flicker of a shadow, nothing that could have warned me—nothing except the inexplicable danger bell that clanged within my brain.

I wheeled about in frantic haste, and it was almost upon me, black in the shadow, man-sized, man-shaped, coming in a rush without the slightest sound. As if it trod on air so it would make no sound to cancel out the sound of footsteps.

I moved so suddenly that I spun back against the wall and the thing rushed past me but pivoted with a whiplash swiftness and launched itself toward me. I caught the paleness of a face as the faint lights of the stairwell outlined the massive body. Without conscious thought, my fist was coming up, aiming at the paleness in the black outline. There was a spattering smack as the fist slammed against the paleness, and my knuckles stung with the violence of the blow.

The man, if it were a man, was staggering back, and I followed, swinging once again, and once again there was the hollow smack.

The man was going over, falling, the small of his back caught against the iron railing that protected the open stairwell above the flight below—pivoting over the rail and falling free, spread-eagled, into the gaping space above the marble stairs.

I caught one glimpse of the face as it turned into the light, the mouth wide open for the scream that did not come. Then the man had fallen out of sight and there was a heavy thud as he smashed onto the staircase a dozen feet below.

There had been fear and desperation when I had faced the man, and now there was a sickness from knowing that I had killed a man. For no one, I told myself, could have survived the fall and landing on the staircase stone.

I stood and waited for a sound to come up from the stairwell. But there was no sound. The building was so still that it seemed to hold its breath.

I moved toward the stairs and my knees were shaky and my hands were clammy. At the railing, I looked down, braced for the sight of the sprawling body which must He broken on the stairs.

And there was nothing there.

There was no sign of the man who had fallen to almost certain death.

I whirled around and went clattering down the stairs, no longer intent on maintaining silence. And mingled with the relief at not having killed a man there was a vague beginning of another fear—that, having failed to kill him, he still remained a stalker and an enemy.

Even as I ran, I wondered if I might have been mistaken, if the body might have been there and my eyes had missed it. But one, I told myself, does not miss a body broken on the stairs.

I was right. The stairs were empty as I came around the first flight and started down the second.

Now I stopped my running and went more cautiously, staring at the treads, as if by doing this I might catch some clue as to exactly what had happened.

And as I came down the stairs, I smelled the lotion smell again— the same scent I had caught on Bennett and in the office, where I'd found Bennett's doll.

There was a smear of liquid, thinly spread, on the first steps and on the landing floor—as if someone had spilled some water. I stooped and ran my fingers through the wetness and it was simply wetness. I lifted my fingers and smelled of them, and the lotion smell was there, but stronger than it had been before.

I could see that two trails of wetness ran across the landing and went down the following flight, as if someone had carried a glass of water and the water had been dripping. This, then, I told myself, was the track of the one who should have died; this wetness was the trail that he had left behind him.

There was horror in that stairwell, a place so quiet and empty that it would have seemed that any emotion, even horror, would have been impossible. But the emptiness itself, perhaps, was a por-tion of the horror, the emptiness where there should have been a body, and the trail of smelly liquid to show the way that it had gone.

I went charging down the stairs, with the horror howling in my brain, and as I ran I wondered what I'd do or what would happen should I meet that shape, waiting on the stairs; but, even thinking of it, I could not halt my fleeing and went hammering down the stairs until I reached the ground floor.

There was no one on the floor except the shoe-shine boy, dozing in a chair tipped back against the wall, and the cigar-counter man, who leaned against the counter, reading a paper he had spread flat before him.

The cigar man looked up and the shoe-shine boy crashed forward in his chair, but before either of them could move or shout, I was through the revolving door and outside on the street. The street was becoming crowded with shoppers, who flocked downtown two nights each week for the evening store hours.

Once in the street, I ran no longer, for here I felt that I might be safe. At the corner, I stopped and looked back at the McCandless Building, and it was just a building, an old and time-stained building that had stood too long and would be torn down before too many years had passed. There was nothing mysterious about it, nothing sinister.

But as I looked at it I shivered, as if a cold wind had come out of somewhere to blow across my soul.

I knew just what I needed and I went down the street to find it. The place was just beginning to fill up, and somewhere in the dimness toward the back someone was playing a piano. Well, not really playing it, just fooling around, every once in a while fingering a snatch of melody.

I went toward the back, where there wasn't so much traffic, and found myself a stool.

"What'll it be?" asked the man behind the bar.

"Scotch on ice," I said. "And while you're about it, you might make it double. It'll save wear and tear on you."

"What brand?" he asked.

I told him.

He got a glass and ice. He picked a bottle off the back bar. Someone sat down on the stool that was next to mine. "Good evening, miss," the bartender said. "What can we do for you?"

"A Manhattan, please."

I turned around at the sound of the voice, for there was something in it that jerked me to attention.

And something about the girl as well.

She was a stunning person, with a beauty that did not erase her personality.

She stared back at me. She was as cool as ice.

"Have we met somewhere?" she asked.

"I believe we have," I told her.

She was the blonde I had picked out of the shoe box—now incredibly grown up and clothed.

12

The bartender set my drink before me and began fixing her Manhattan.

He had a bored look on his face. He'd heard a lot of pick-ups made, most likely, at this very bar.

"Not too long ago," she said.

"No." I told her. "Just a little time. At an office, I believe."

If she knew what I was talking about, she surely didn't show it. And yet she was too cold, too icy, too sure of herself.

She opened a cigarette case and took out a smoke. She tapped it and stuck it in her mouth and waited.

"I'm sorry," I told her. "I don't smoke. I don't carry fire."

She reached into her bag and took out a lighter. She handed it to me. I snapped it and the flame licked out. She leaned to get the light, and as she did I smelled the scent of violets—or, at least, of some floral perfume. I imagined it was violet.

And suddenly I became aware of something I should have thought of at the very first. Bennett had not smelled the way he did because he had used shaving lotion but because he had failed to use it. The scent of him had been the smell of the sort of thing he was.

The girl got her light and leaned back, dragging in the first lungful of the smoke. She let it trickle from her nostrils very daintily.

I handed her the lighter. She dropped it in her bag.

"Thank you, sir," she said.

The bartender put her Manhattan on the bar. It was a pretty thing, with the stemmed red cherry exactly positioned.

I gave him a bill.

"The both of them," I said.

"But, sir," she protested.

"Don't thwart me," I pleaded. "It's a passion with me—providing pretty girls with booze."

She let it pass. She eyed me, still a little coldly.

"You've never smoked?" she asked.

I shook my head.

"To keep your sense of smell?" she asked.

"My what?"

"Your sense of smell. I thought you might be in some sort of work where a sense of smell might be an asset."

"I had never thought of it that way," I said, "but perhaps I am."

She picked up her drink and looked at me closely above the top of it.

"Sir," she said calmly, evenly, "would you like to sell yourself?"

I'm afraid that that one got me. I didn't even stammer. I just stared at her. For she wasn't kidding; she was business-like.

"We could start at a million" she said, "and bargain up from there."

I got my mental feet back under me again. "My soul?" I asked. "Or is the body all? With the soul, it would come just a little higher."

"You could keep your soul," she told me.

"And the offer comes from you?"

She shook her head. "Not me. I have no use of you."

"You represent someone? Someone, perhaps, who'd buy anything at all. A store and close it down. Or an entire city."

"You catch on fast," she said.

"Money's not everything," I told her. "There are other things."

"If you prefer," she said, "we could consider other things."

She put down her drink and reached into her bag. She handed me a card.

"If you should reconsider, you can hunt me up," she said. "The offer's still wide open."

She was off the stool and moving out into the gathering crowd before I could answer or do a thing to stop her.

The bartender drifted past and looked at the untouched drinks.

"Something wrong with the liquor, bud?" he asked.

"Not a thing," I told him.

I put the card on the bar and it was upside down. I turned it over and bent above it to make out what it said, because the light was dim.

I needn't have read it. I already knew what it would say. There was one difference only, in a single line. Instead of "Property Management," it said "We Deal in Everything."

I sat there cold and huddled, perched upon the stool. The place was so dim that it had a foggy look, and there was a rumble of disconnected human talk that somehow sounded not too human but like the gabbling of monsters or the hoots of idiots. And through it, and above it, and in between the talk, the piano still was tinkling like a dirty joke.

I gulped the Scotch and sat there with the glass cradled in my hand. I looked around for the man behind the bar to get another one, but he had suddenly gotten busy with new customers.

Someone leaned on the bar beside me, and his elbow jogged the Manhattan and the glass went over. The drink spread out like a coat of dirty oil across the polished wood and the stem of the glass snapped off close up against the bowl and the bowl was shattered. The cherry rolled along the bar and stopped at its very edge.

"I'm sorry," said the man. "It was clumsy of me. I'll buy another one."

"Never mind," I told him. "She isn't coming back."

I slid off the stool and made it to the door.

A cab was cruising past, and I stepped out and hailed it.

13

The last light of the day had faded from the sky and the streetlights were on. I saw that a clock set up on a corner in front of a bank said it was almost six-thirty. I'd have to get a hustle on, for I had a date at seven and Joy, more than likely, would be fairly well burned up if I should turn up late.

"Going to be a great night for coon hunting," said the cabby. "It is warm and soft, and in just a little while the moon will be coming up. I wish I could get out, but I got to work tonight. Me and another fellow, we have got a dog. A black and tan. He has got the sweetest mouth that you've ever listened to."

"You're a coon hunter," I said, making it half a question, but not entirely so. Not that I was interested, but it was clear the man expected some reaction from me.

It was all he needed. Probably all he had expected.

"Been one man and boy," he told me. "My old pappy, he use to take me out when I was nine or ten years old. I tell you, mister, it gets into your blood. Come a night like this and you can hardly stand it, wanting to be out there. There's something about the way the woods smell at this time of year and there's the special noise the wind makes in the trees when the leaves are loosening and you can feel the frost just around the corner."

"Where do you go to hunt?"

"Out west, forty or fifty miles. Up the river. Lots of timber in the river bottom."

"You get lots of coons?"

"Ain't the coons you get," he said. "Lots of nights you go out and you come back with nothing. The coons maybe are just an excuse for getting out in the woods at night. There ain't enough people get out into the woods, at night or any other time. I ain't the kind of guy that goes around spouting about communing with nature, but I tell you, friend, if you spent some time with her, you're a better man."

I settled back in the seat and watched the blocks slide past. It was still the same old city I had known, and yet it seemed to me that now there was a leering quality about it, as if sly shapes might be peering out at one from the shadowed angles of the darkened buildings.

The driver asked me: "You never went coon hunting?"

"No, I never have. I do some duck hunting and sometimes go out to South Dakota for the pheasants."

"Yeah," he said, "I like ducks and pheasants, too. But when you come to coons, they are something special."

He was silent for a moment, and then he said: "I guess, though, it's each man to his own. With you it's ducks and pheasants and with me it's coons. And I know a man, a real gone old geezer, that messes around with skunks. He don't think there's nothing like a skunk. He makes friends with them. I swear he talks to them. He clucks and coos at them and they walk right up to him and climb up in his lap and let him pet them like a cat. Then, like as not, they go trailing home with him, like a happy dog. I tell you, it is unbelievable. It would scare you to see how he gets along with them. He lives in a shack out in the river hills and the place plumb crawls with skunks. He's writing a book about them. He showed me the book. He's writing it with pencil on a common dime-store tablet—the rough kind of paper that kids use at school. He sits there hunched over the table with a stub of a pencil he has to lick every now and then when it gets too faint, writing away at that book in the light of a smoky old lantern setting on the table. But, I tell you, mister, he can't write for shucks and his spelling's something terrible. And it's a downright pity. For he's got a book to write."

"That's the way it goes," I told him.

He drove along in silence for a while.

"Your place next block, isn't it?" he asked.

I told him that it was.

He pulled up in front of the apartment and I got out.

"Some night," he said, "how about a coon hunt with me? Start six o'clock or so."

"That would be fine," I said.

"The name is Larry Higgins. You'll find me in the phone book. Call me any time."

I told him that I would.

14

I climbed the stairs, and in front of my door someone had replaced the semicircle that had been cut out of the carpeting. I almost didn't notice it because the light bulb in the ceiling was dimmer, if possible, than it had been before.

I almost stepped into the semicircle before I saw the carpet had been mended. I wasn't thinking about the carpeting. There was too much else for a man to think about.

I stopped at the very edge of it and stood there stiffly, as a man may stand who toes a dangerous deadline. And the funny thing about it was that it was not new carpeting, but the same old worn, dirty carpeting as all the rest of it.

Was it possible, I wondered, that the caretaker could have found, hidden in some cranny, the very piece that had been cut out of the carpeting?

I got down on my knees to have a look at it and there was no sign at all that the carpet had been cut. It was as if a man had only imagined that the carpet had been cut. There was no sign of sewing and there weren't any seams.

I ran my hand over the area where the semicircle once had been and it was carpeting. It wasn't any phony paper spread across at trap.

I felt the texture of it and the yielding thickness of it, and there was no doubt at all that it was honest fabric.

And yet I was leery of it. It had almost fooled me once and I was not inclined to let it fool me once again. I stayed there, kneeling in the hall, and above me and behind me I heard the tiny, gnatlike singing of the light bulb in the ceiling.

Slowly I got to my feet and found the key and leaned across that space of carpeting to unlock the door. Anyone who saw me would have thought that I was crazy—standing just off-center of the hall and leaning across all that space to get the door unlocked.

The lock snicked back and the door came open and I leaped across the space of replaced carpeting, never touching it, and was inside the room.

I closed the door behind me and stood with my back against it as I turned on the light.

And the room was there, waiting for me as it always waited, a place that spelled security and comfort, the place that was my home.

But a place, I reminded myself, that would continue to be my home for somewhat less than another ninety days.

And after that? I wondered. What would happen then, not only to myself, but to all those other people? What would happen to the city?

"We Deal in Everything," the card had said. Like the old junk dealer who bought anything at all—bottles, bones, rags, anything you had. But the junk dealer had been an honest buyer. He had bought for profit. And what were these people buying for? Why was Fletcher Atwood buying? Not for profit, certainly, when he paid more than a business might be worth and then didn't even use it.

I took off my coat and threw it in a chair. I threw my hat on top of it. At the desk I dug out the phone directory and turned the pages to the Atwoods. There were a lot of them, but no Fletcher Atwood. There wasn't any Atwood, even, who had an F initial.

So I dialed information.

She had a look then told me, in her singsong voice: "We have no such party listed."

I hung up the phone and wondered what to do.

Here was an emergency that cried aloud for action, and how did one get action? And if you got the action, what would the action be? What do you do, what can you do, if someone buys a city?

And, first of all, how would you explain it so someone would believe you?

I ran through the list of names and none of them was hopeful. There was the Old Man, of course, and he was the one I should spill my guts to, if for no other reason than that I worked for him. But if I should even hint at what was happening, he probably would fire me as a rank incompetent.

There were the mayor and the police chief or possibly some judicial officer, like the county prosecutor or the attorney general, but if I even breathed it to any one of them, I would either get a quick brush-off as another crackpot or find myself locked up.

There was always, I told myself, Senator Roger Hill. Rog just might listen to me.

I put out my hand to pick up the phone, then pulled it back again.

When I got through to Washington, what exactly was it that I had to tell him?

I reviewed it in my mind: "Look, Rog, someone is trying to buy up the city. I broke into an office and I found the papers and there was this rack of clothes and a shoe box full of dolls and a big hole in the wall . . ."

It was too ridiculous to even think about, too fantastic to hope that anyone would take it seriously. If someone had tried to tell me that sort of story, I would have figured he was some kind of nut or other.

Before I went to anyone, I had to get more evidence. I had to nail it down. I had to be able to show who and how and why and I had to do it fast. There was a place to start and that was Fletcher

Atwood. Wherever he might be, he was the man to find. I knew two solid things about him. He had no telephone and years ago he'd bought the Belmont place out on Timber Lane. There was some question, of course, that he had ever lived there, but it would be a place to start. Even if Atwood were not there, even if he never had been there, it was possible one would find something in the house that might be a help in picking up his trail.

My watch said that it was a quarter of seven and I had to pick up Toy and there was no time to change. I'd just put on a clean shirt and pick out a different tie and Joy wouldn't mind. After all, we weren't out to paint the town; we were only going out to eat.

I went into the bedroom without bothering to turn on the light, for the lamp in the living room threw a shaft of light clear across the bedroom. I pulled open a dresser drawer and got a shirt. I stripped off the plastic cover that the laundry had put on and pulled out the cardboard. I shook out the shirt and threw it across a chair back, then went to the closet to pick out a tie. And even as I was pulling the knob on the closet door, I realized that I'd not turned on the light and that I'd need to turn it on before I could pick out a tie.

I had the door open, perhaps a foot or so, and as I thought about the light I shut the door again. I don't know why I did it. I could just as easily have left it open while I crossed the room to trip up the light switch.

And in that instant of opening and closing the door, which took less time than it takes to tell it, I saw or sensed or heard—I don't know which it was—the movement of some sort of life inside the darkness of the closet. As if the clothes had come to life and had been waiting for me; as if the ties, hanging on their racks, had metamorphosed into snakes, hanging motionless, as ties, until it came the time to strike.

Had I waited for the sensing or the seeing or the hearing of that motion in the closet to slam shut the door, it might have been to late. But the motion in the closet had not a thing to do with my shutting of the door. I had already started to push it shut again before there was any motion—or, at least, before I had become aware of it.

I backed away across the room from the terror that writhed behind the door, with horror welling in me—the bubbling, effervescent horror that can only come when a man's own home develops fangs against him.

And even as the horror chilled me, I argued with myself—for this was the sort of thing that simply could not happen. A man's chair may develop jaws and snap him up as he bends to sit in it; his scatter rugs may glide treacherously from beneath his feet; his refrigerator may lie in ambush to topple over on him; but the closet is the place where nothing of the sort can happen. For the closet is a part of the man himself. It is the place where he hangs up his artificial pelts, and as such it is closer to him, more intimate with him than any room within his dwelling place.

But even as I told myself that it could not happen, even as I charged it all against an upset imagination, I could hear the rustling and the sliding and the frantic stealth that was going on behind the closet door.

Almost reluctantly, strange as it may sound, half held by a deadly fascination, I backed out of the room and stood in the living room, just beyond the bedroom door, staring back into the darkness and the slithering. And there was something there: unless I doubted all my senses and my sanity, there was something there.

Something, I told myself, that was a piece with the trap beneath the carpet camouflage and with the ordinary shoe box filled with extraordinary dolls.

And why me? I wondered. Since the incident of the dolls and the broken office door and the girl who ordered the Manhattan, it could, of course, logically be me. Stemming from those happenings, I well could be a target. But the trap had been the first—the trap had come before any of the others.

I strained my ears to hear the rustling, but either it had quieted down now that I was gone or I was too far from the closet, for I did not hear it.

I went to the gun cabinet and unlocked the drawer underneath the cabinet and found the automatic. I dug out a box of shells and filled the clip and shoved it home. I dumped out into my hand the cartridges remaining in the box and dropped them in my pocket.

I put on my topcoat and eased the automatic into my right-hand pocket. Then I hunted for my car keys. For I was getting out.

The keys weren't in the topcoat and they weren't in my jacket or in the pockets of my trousers. I had my key ring, with the keys to the front door and to the gun cabinet, to my office desk, to my safety-deposit box, plus half a dozen others that belonged to locks long since forgotten—the steady, ridiculous, inevitable collection of useless and forgotten keys that one can never quite bring himself to throw away.

I had all these, but I didn't have the car keys.

I searched the tabletops and the desk. I went into the kitchen and had a look around. There weren't any keys.

Standing in the kitchen, I knew just where I'd left them. I knew just where they were. I could see the trunk key and the caddy dangling from the dash, with the ignition key stuck neatly into the ignition lock. When I'd come home that afternoon, I'd left them in the car. Just as sure as shooting, I'd left them in the car, and it was something I almost never did.

I started for the front door. I took two steps and stopped. And I knew, as certainly as I stood there, that I could not go out into the darkness of the parking lot and walk up to the car with the keys already in the lock.

It was illogical. It was crazy. But I couldn't help it. There was no way to help it. With no keys in the lock—OK, I could have gone out to the lot. But the keys' hanging in the lock, for some strange, totally illogical, and unknown reason, made a terrifying difference.

I was scared stiff and toothless. I found my hands were shaking, and I hadn't even realized it until I looked at them.

The clock said it was seven and Joy would be waiting. She'd be waiting and she'd be sore and I couldn't blame her.

"Not a minute later," she had told me. "I get hungry early."

I walked to the desk and stretched out my hand to pick up the phone, but my hand stopped short of touching it. For a sudden terrifying thought came thundering through my brain. What if the phone no longer were a phone? What if nothing in this room were what it appeared to be? What if it all had changed in the last few minutes into booby traps?

I reached into my pocket and pulled out the automatic. I pushed tentatively at the phone with the snout of it and the phone did not erupt into a funny kind of life. It remained a phone.

With the gun still clutched in one hand, I picked up the receiver with the other, laid it on the desk, and dialed the number.

And when I picked up the receiver, I wondered what I'd say.

It was simple enough. I told her who I was.

"What's keeping you?" she asked just a mite too sweetly.

"Joy, I'm in trouble."

"What's the matter this time?"

Only kidding me. I seldom was in trouble.

"I mean real trouble," I told her. "Dangerous trouble. I can't take you out tonight."

"Sissy," she said. "I'll come and get you."

"Joy!" I shouted. "Listen! For God's sake, listen to me. Keep away from me. Believe me, I know what I'm doing. Just stay away from me."

Her voice still was calm, but it had tightened up a bit, it seemed. "What's the matter, Parker? Just what kind of trouble?"

"I don't know," I told her desperately. "There is something going on. Something dangerous and funny. You wouldn't believe me if I told you. No one would believe me. I'll work it out, but I don't want you to get mixed up in it. I'll feel like a fool tomorrow, maybe, but—"

"Parker, are you sober?"

I told her: "I wish to God I weren't."

"And you're all right? Right now, you are all right?"

"I'm all right," I told her. "But there's something in the closet and there was a trap outside the door and I found a box of dolls . . ."

I stopped, and I could have cut out my tongue for saying what I had. I hadn't meant to say it.

"Stay right there," she said. "I'll be there in a minute."

"Joy!" I shouted. "Joy, don't do it!"

But the phone was dead.

Desperately I hung up and lifted the receiver again to dial her number.

The crazy little fool, I thought. I had to get her stopped.

I could hear the ringing. It rang on and on and there was a terrible emptiness in the sound it made. It rang and rang and rang and there was no answer.

I shouldn't have said what I said, I told myself. I should have pretended that I was stinking drunk and in no shape to take her out and that would have made her sore and more than likely she'd have hung up on me and it would have been all right. Or maybe I should have thought up some story with at least the sound of plausibility, but there had been no time to think up a really good one. I was too scared to think straight. I still was too scared to think straight.

I put the receiver back into its cradle and grabbed up my hat and started for the door. At the door I stopped for an instant and looked back into the room, and now it had an alien look, as if it were a place I had never seen before, a place I had merely stumbled on, and it was full of slithering and of whispering and almost-silent noise.

I jerked the door open and bolted out into the corridor and went thundering down the stairs. And even as I ran I wondered how much of the almost-silent, stealthy noise I'd heard had actually been in the apartment and how much in my head.

I reached the lobby and went out onto the sidewalk. The night was quiet and soft and there was the smell of leaf smoke in the air.

From up the street came a clicking noise—a queer, rapid, rhythmic clicking—and around the corner of the building, out of the alley that led to the parking lot, came a dog. He was a happy dog, for his tail was wagging and his gait had something close to frolic in it. He was half the size of a horse and so shaggy that he was shapeless and it was almost as if he'd come straight out of the autumn sunlight of that very afternoon.

"Hi, pup," I said, and he came up to me and sat down happily and beat his ponderous tail in doggish ecstasy upon the concrete of the sidewalk.

I put out my hand to pat his head, but I never got it patted, for a car came humming swiftly down the street and swung in sharply to stop in front of us.

The door came open.

"Get in," said Joy's voice, "and let's get out of here."

15

We ate in another world of candlelight, one of those crazy, corny places that Joy seemed to love—not at the new night-club that was opening out on Pinecrest Drive. That is, Joy ate. I didn't.

Women are the damnedest people. I told her all about it. I'd already told her so much over the telephone, inadvisedly perhaps, that I had to tell her the rest of it. Actually, of course, there was no reason that I shouldn't tell her, but I sounded sappy doing it. She went ahead and ate, in her sweet, calm way, as if I'd been telling her no more than the latest office gossip.

It was almost as if she hadn't believed a word of what I said, although I am sure she did. Maybe she saw I was upset (who wouldn't be upset?) and was simply doing her womanly duty of getting me calmed down.

"Go ahead and eat, Parker," she told me. "No matter what is going on, you simply have to eat."

I looked at my plate and gagged.

At just the thought of food, not at what was on the plate. In the candlelight there was no way of telling what was on the plate.

"Joy," I asked her, "why was I afraid to go out into the parking lot?"

That was the thing that bothered me. That was the thing that hurt.

"Because you're a coward," she said.

She wasn't helping any.

I dabbled at my food. It tasted the way you'd expect food you couldn't see to taste.

The tiny, tinny orchestra struck up another tune—the kind of tune that went with a place like that.

I looked around the room and thought about the slithering sound that had come from behind the closet door, and it was impossible, of course. Sitting here, in this kind of atmosphere, it could be nothing more than a thing snatched naked from the middle of a dream.

But it was there, I knew. It was true, I knew. Outside the cloying, muffling influence of this man-made feather bed, there was a stark reality that no one yet had faced. That I had touched, or glimpsed, perhaps, but no more than the very edge of it.

"What," Joy asked me, reading my thoughts, "do you intend to do about it?"

"I don't know," I said.

"You're a newspaperman," she told me, "and there's a story out there waiting for you. But, Parker, please be careful."

"Oh certainly," I said.

"What do you think it is?"

I shook my head,

"You don't believe it," I said. "I don't see, this minute, how anyone can believe it."

"I believe your own interpretation of it. But it is your interpretation right?"

"It's the only one I have."

"You were drunk that first night. Blind, stinking drunk, you said. The trap—"

"But there was the cutout carpeting. I saw that when I was bright sober. And the office—"

"Let's take it step by step," she said. "Let's get it figured out. You can't let it throw you. You can't let it bowl you over."

"That is it!" I shouted.

For I had forgotten.

"Don't shout," she said. "You'll have people looking at us."

"The bowling balls," I told her. "I had forgotten them. There were bowling balls rolling down the road."

"Parker!"

"Out in Timber Lane. Joe Newman called me."

I saw her face across the table and I saw that she was scared. She'd taken all the rest of it, but the bowling balls had been the final straw. She thought that I was crazy.

"I'm sorry," I said as gently as I could.

"But, Parker! Bowling balls rolling down the road!"

"One behind the other. Rolling solemnly."

"And Joe Newman saw them?"

"No, not Joe. Some high-school kids. They phoned in and Joe called me. I told him to forget it."

"Out by the Belmont place?"

"That's just it," I said. "It all ties in, you see. I don't know how, but somehow it all is tied together."

I pushed the plate away and shoved back the chair.

"Where are you going, Parker?"

"First," I told her, "I'm going to take you home. And, then, if you'll loan me the car . . ."

"Certainly, but—oh, I see, the Belmont place."

16

The Belmont house was dark, a huge, rectangular blackness reared among the blackness of the trees. It stood upon a high point of land thrust out into the lake, and when I stopped the car I could hear the running of the waves upon the beach. Through the trees I could see the glint of moonlight on the water and high up, in a gable, a window caught the light, but otherwise the house and its sentinel trees were wrapped in blackness. The rustling of the drying leaves, heard in the silence of the night, sounded like the furtive pattering of many little feet.

I got out of the car and closed the door, gently so it wouldn't bang. And once I got the door shut, I stayed standing there, looking at the house. I wasn't scared exactly. The terror and the horror of the early evening had largely ebbed away. But I didn't feel too brave.

There might be traps, I thought. Not the kind of trap that had been hidden just outside my door, but other kinds of traps. Very fiendish ones.

And then I chided myself for that kind of foolishness. For simple logic said there'd be no traps outside. For if there were, they'd catch the innocent—someone cutting through the property to get down to the lake, or children playing around that most attractive of all childish things, a vacant house—and thus would attract attention where none need be attracted. If there were any traps, they'd be inside the house. And even so, thinking of it, that seemed unlikely, too. For on their own home grounds they—whoever *they* might be—could deal with an intruder without resorting to traps.

It probably was no more, I told myself, than errant foolishness, this whole idea of mine that the Belmont house was in some way connected with what was going on. And yet I had to go and see, I had to know, I had to run it to the end and eliminate it, or I'd always wonder if the clues had not been there.

I went tensely up the walk, my shoulders hunched against possible attack from an unknown quarter. I tried to unhunch them, but they stayed tightened up no matter how I tried.

I climbed the steps to the front door and stood there, hesitating, debating with myself. And decided, finally, to do it the honest way, to ring the bell or knock. I hunted for the bell and found it in the darkness by the sense of touch. The button was loose and wobbled underneath my fingers and I knew it wasn't working, but I pressed it just the same. I could hear no sound of ringing from inside the house. I pressed it once again and held it there, and there was still no sound of ringing. I knocked, and the knocking sounded loud in the quietness of the night.

I waited and nothing happened. Once I thought I heard a footfall, but it was not repeated, and I knew that it could be no more than my imagination.

Back down the steps, I moved around the house. Uncared for through many years, the foundation plantings had grown into thick, dense hedges. Fallen leaves rustled underfoot and there was a queer, almost acid autumn sharpness in the air.

The screen was loose in the fifth window that I tried. And the window was unlocked.

And it was easy, I thought—far too easy. If I were looking for a trap, here could be the trap.

I raised the window to the top and waited, and nothing happened. There was no sound except the sound of the waves upon the shore and the noisy walking of the wind through the dry leaves still hanging in the trees. I put my hand into my topcoat pocket and the gun was there, and the flashlight I had taken from the glove compartment of Joy's car.

I waited a little longer, getting up my nerve. Then I boosted myself through the open window.

I stepped quickly to one side, with my back against the wall, so that I wouldn't be outlined against the window opening. I stood there for a while, straight against the wall, trying to hold in my breathing so I'd catch the slightest sound.

Nothing happened. Nothing moved. And there was no sound.

I lifted the flashlight out of my pocket and switched it on and swept the room with its shaft of light. There was dust-sheeted furniture, there were paintings on the wall, there was a trophy of some sort standing on the fireplace mantel.

I switched off the light and slid swiftly along the wall, just on the chance that someone or something had been hiding among the sheeted furniture and might decide to have a go at me.

Nothing did.

I waited some more.

The room went on being nothing but a room.

I soft-footed across it and went out into the entrance hall. I found the kitchen and the dining room and a study, where empty bookshelves gaped back at me like an old man with a toothless grin.

I didn't find a thing.

The dust was heavy on the floor and I left tracks across it. The furniture all was sheeted. The place held a slightly musty smell. It had the feel of a house that had been left behind, a house that people had unaccountably walked away from and then never had come back to.

I had been a fool to come, I told myself. There was nothing here. I had simply allowed my imagination to run away with me.

But so long as I was here, I figured, I should make a job of it. Foolish as it all had been, it would be senseless to leave until I had seen the rest of the house, the upstairs and the basement.

I trailed back to the entry hall and started up the staircase, a spiral affair with gleaming rail and posts.

I had gotten three treads up when the voice stopped me.

"Mr. Graves," it said.

It was a smooth and cultivated voice and it spoke in normal tones. And while it had some question in it, it was conversational. It brought my hair up straight, stiff upon my head, prickling at my scalp.

I spun around, scrabbling for the gun weighing down my pocket.

I had it halfway out when the voice spoke again.

"I'm Atwood," said the voice. "I'm sorry that the bell is broken."

"I also knocked," I said.

"I didn't hear your knock. I was downstairs working."

I could see him now, a dark figure in the hall. I let the gun slide back into the pocket.

"We could go downstairs," said Atwood, "and have a pleasant talk. This hardly is the place for an extended conversation."

"If you wish," I told him.

I came down the stairs and he led the way, down the hall and to the basement door. Light flooded up the stairway and I saw him now. He was a most ordinary-looking man, the quiet, pleasant, business type.

"I like it down here," said Atwood, going easily and unconcern-edly down the stairs. "The former owner fixed up this amusement room, which to my mind is far more livable than any other part of the house. I suppose that may be because the rest of the house is old and the room down here is a fairly new addition."

We reached the bottom of the stairs and turned the corner and were in the amusement room.

It was a large place, running the entire length of the basement, with a fireplace at each end and some furniture scattered here and there on the red tile floor. A table stood against one wall, its top lit-tered with papers; opposite the table, in the outer wall, was a hole— a round hole bored into the wall, about the size to accommodate a bowling ball—and from it a cold wind swept and blew across my ankles. And there was in the air, as well, the faintest suggestion of the shaving lotion smell.

Out of the corner of my eye, I saw Atwood watching me, and I tried to freeze my face—not into a frozen mask, but into the kind of mask that I imagined was my everyday appearance. And I must have done it, for there was no smile on Atwood's face, as there might have been if he'd trapped me into some expression of bewilderment or fear.

"You are right," I told him. "It is very livable."

I said it simply to be saying something. For the place was not livable, not by human standards. Dust lay almost as deep in this room as it had upstairs, and there was small junk of all descriptions scattered all about and stacked into the corners.

"Won't you have a chair?" said Atwood. He waved toward a deeply cushioned one that stood slantwise of the table.

I walked across the floor to reach it and the floor rustled underneath my feet. Looking down, I saw that I had walked across a large sheet of almost transparent plastic that lay crumpled on the floor.

"Something that the former owner left," said Atwood carelessly. "Someday I'll have to get around to cleaning up the place."

I sat down in the chair.

"Your coat," said Atwood.

"I believe that I will keep it. There seems to be a draft in here."

I watched his face and there was no expression in it.

"You catch on quick," said Atwood, but there was no menace in this tone. "Perhaps a bit too quick."

I said nothing and he said, "Although I'm glad you came. It is not often that one meets a man of your fine perception."

I kidded him: "Meaning that you're about to offer me a job in your organization?"

"The thought," said Atwood quietly, "has passed across my mind."

I shook my head. "I doubt you have any need of me. You've already done a fair job of buying up the city."

"City!" Atwood cried, outraged.

I nodded at him.

He spun a chair out from the desk and sat down carefully.

"I see that you do not comprehend," he told me. "I must put you right."

"Please do," I told him. "That is what I'm here for."

Atwood leaned forward earnestly.

"Not the city," he said quietly, tensely. "You must not sell me short. Far more than a city, Mr. Graves. Much more than a city. I think it's safe to say it, for now no one can stop me. I am buying up the Earth!"

17

There are some ideas so monstrous, so perverted, so outrageous that one's mind must take a little time to become accustomed to them.

And one of these ideas is that anyone should even think of trying to buy up the Earth. Conquer it—most certainly, for that is an old and fine and traditional idea that has been held by many men. Destroy it—that also is understandable, for there have been madmen who have used the threat of such destruction as an adjunct, if not the backbone, of their policy.

But buying it was unthinkable.

First of all, it was impossible, for no one had the money. And even if one had, it still was crazy—for what would one do with it once one got it bought? And, thirdly, it was unethical and a perversion of tradition, for one does not kill off utterly all his competitors if he's a businessman. He may absorb them, or control them, but he does not kill them off.

Atwood sat there, poised on the edge of his chair, like an anxious hawk, and he must have read some censure into my very silence.

"There's nothing wrong with it," he told me. "It is entirely legal."

"I suppose there's not," I said. Although I knew there was. If only I could have pulled the words together, I could have told him what was wrong with it.

"We are operating," Atwood said, "within the human structure. We are operating within and abiding by your rules and regulations. Not only the rules and regulations, but even by your customs. We have violated not a single one of them. And I tell you, my friend, that is not an easy thing. It is rare that one can operate without violating custom."

I tried to get some words out, but they gurgled in my throat and died. It was just as well. I was not even sure what I had meant to say.

"There's nothing wrong," said Atwood, "with our money or our securities."

"Just one thing," I said. "You have too much money, far too much of it."

But it was not the idea of too much money that was bothering me. It was something else. Something far more important than having too much money.

It was the words he used and the way he used them. The way he said "our" to include himself and whoever was leagued with him; the way he used "your" to include all the world exclusive of his group. And the stress he'd put upon the fact that he had operated within the human structure.

It was as if my brain had split in two. As if one side of it shouted horror and the other pleaded reason. For the idea was too monstrous to even think about.

He was grinning at me now and I was filled with sudden rage. The shouting of the one side of my brain drowned out the reason and I came out of the chair, with my hand snaking the gun out of my pocket.

I would have shot him in that instant. Without mercy, without thinking, I would have shot to kill. Like stamping on a snake, like swatting at a fly—it was no more than that.

But I didn't get the chance to shoot.

For Atwood came unstuck.

I don't know how to tell it. There is no way to tell it. It was something that no human had ever seen before. There are no words in any human language for the thing that Atwood did.

He didn't fade or flicker. He didn't suddenly melt down. Whatever it was he did, he did it all at once.

One second he was sitting there. And the next second he was gone. I didn't see him go.

There was a tiny click, as if someone had dropped a light metallic object, and there was a flock of jet-black bowling balls that had not been there before bouncing on the floor.

My mind must have gone through certain acrobatics, but I was not aware of them. What I did, I seemed to do instinctively, without even thinking of it—unaware of the interplay of cause and effect, of fact, surmise, and hunch that must have gone flashing through my brain to spur me into action.

I dropped the gun and stooped, grabbing up the sheet of plastic off the floor. And even as I grabbed it and began to shake it out, I moved toward the outer wall, heading for the hole from which blew the chilly breeze.

The bowling balls were coming at me, heading for the hole, and I was ready for them, with the plastic centered on the hole, a trap that waited for them.

The first one hit the hole and drove the plastic in and the second followed close behind—and the third and fourth and fifth.

I made a grab to bring, the ends of the plastic sheet together and pulled it from the hole, and inside of it the jet-black bowling balls clicked excitedly as they knocked together.

There were others of them rolling in that basement room—the ones that had been scared off and had escaped the net and now were rolling frantically, seeking for a place to hide.

I lifted up the bag of plastic and gave it a shake to settle the balls I'd caught well into its bottom. I twisted the neck of plastic tightly to hold them in and swung the bag thus formed across my shoulders. And all around me ran the whispering and the slithering as the other balls sought for shadowed corners.

"All right," I yelled at them, "back into your hole! Back to where you came from!"

But there was no answer. They all were hidden now. Hidden in the shadow and among the junk and watching me from there. Not seeing me, perhaps. More like sensing, likely. But, no matter how they did it, watching.

I took a forward step and my foot came down on something. I jumped in sudden fright.

It was nothing but my gun, lying on the floor, dropped when I had grabbed the plastic.

I stood and looked at it and felt the shaking and the trembling that was inside of me, held inside of me and struggling to begin, but unable to begin because my body was too tight and tense to tremble. My teeth were trying to chatter and they couldn't chatter, for my jaws were clamped together with such fanatic desperation that the muscles ached.

There were watchers everywhere and the cold wind blowing from the hole and the excited, not quite angry clicking of the balls in the sack across my shoulder. And the emptiness—the emptiness of a basement where there'd been two men and now was only one. And, worse than that, the howling emptiness of a universe insane and an Earth that had lost its meaning and a culture that now was lost and groping, although it did not know it yet.

Over and above it all was the smell—the scent I'd smelled that morning—the odor of these creatures, whoever they might be, wherever they might come from, whatever was their purpose. But certainly nothing of the Earth, not of our old, familiar planet— nothing that man had ever known before.

I fought against admitting what I knew—that here I faced a life form from outside, from somewhere other than this planet where I at this moment stood. But there was no other answer.

I let the bag down from my shoulder and stooped to scoop up the gun, and as I reached out my fingers for it I saw that something else lay on the floor a little distance from it.

My fingers let the gun go and darted out and picked up this other object, and as they closed upon it I saw it was a doll. Even before I had a chance to look at it, I knew what kind of doll it was, remembering the tiny metallic click I'd heard as Atwood disappeared.

I was right. The doll was Atwood. Every line upon his face, every feature of him, the very feeling of him. As if someone had taken the living Atwood and compressed him to, perhaps, a hundredth of his size, being careful in the process not to change him, not to distort a single atom of the creature that was Atwood.

I dropped the doll into a pocket and grabbed up the gun. Then I straightened to my feet and slung the bag across my shoulder and went across the basement to the stairs.

I wanted to run. It took every ounce of will power that I had to keep my feet from running. But I forced myself to walk. As if I didn't care, as if I weren't scared, as if there were nothing in all God's world or in the universe that could scare a man, that could make him run.

For I had to show them!

Unaccountably, on the spur of the moment, almost as if by instinct, I knew that I had to show them, that I had to act in this instant for all the rest of mankind, that I had to demonstrate the courage and determination and the basic stubbornness that was in the human race.

I don't know how I did it, but I did. I walked across the floor and climbed the stairs, without hurrying, feeling the daggers of their watching pointed at my back. I reached the top of the stairs and closed the door behind me, being careful not to bang it.

Then, free of the watching eyes, free of the need of acting, I stumbled down the hallway and somehow got the front door open and felt the clean sweep of night air from across the lake, cleaning my nostrils and my brain of the stench in the basement room.

I found a tree and leaned against it, weak and winded, as if I'd run a race, and retching, sick to the core and soul of me. I shook and gagged and vomited, and the taste of bile, biting in my throat and mouth, was almost a welcome taste—the taste, somehow, of a basic and a bare humanity.

I stayed there, with my forehead leaning on the roughness of the trunk, and the roughness was a comfort, a contact once again with the world I knew. I heard the booming of the waves upon the lakeshore and the death dance of the leaves, already dead but hanging still upon the parent tree, and from somewhere far off the distance-muffled barking of a dog.

Finally I straightened from the tree and used my sleeve to wipe my mouth and chin. For now it was time to get to doing. Now I had something to support my story, a sack full of things that would support my story, and somehow or other I had to get the story told.

I hoisted the sack back on my shoulder, and as I did so I caught the faint edge of the alien odor once again.

My legs were weak and my gut was sore and I felt cold all over. What I needed more than anything, I told myself, was a slug of booze.

The car was a dark blur in the driveway and I headed for it, none too steady. Behind me the house loomed up, with the moonlight still breaking into sharded silver from the one window, high up in a gable.

A funny thought hit me: I'd left the window open, and maybe I should go back and close it, for the wind could blow leaves into the rooms with their white-shrouded furniture and the rain would drive in on the carpeting and when the snows came there would be little drifts of white running in the room.

I laughed harshly at myself for thinking such a thing when every minute was a minute to be used in getting out and as far away as possible from this house in Timber Lane.

I reached the car and swung open the door next to the wheel. Something stirred in the opposite side of the seat, and it said to me: "I am glad to see you back. I was worrying about how you were getting on."

I froze in unbelieving terror.

For the thing sitting in the seat, the thing that had spoken to me, was the happy, shaggy dog I'd met for the second time that very evening on the sidewalk in front of my apartment house!

18

I see," said the Dog, "that you have one of them. Hang onto it tight. I can testify they're slippery characters."

And he told me that when I had all that I could do to hang on to the edges of my sanity.

I just stood there, I guess. There was nothing else to do. Get belted over the head often enough and you turn sort of dopey.

"Well," said the Dog reprovingly, "it would seem that now's the time for you to ask me who the hell I am."

"All right," I croaked. "Just who the hell are you?"

"Now," said the Dog, delighted, "I am glad you asked me that. For I can tell you frankly that I'm a competitor—I'm sure competitor is the proper term—of the thing you have there in the sack."

"That tells me a lot," I said. "Mister, whoever you may be, you had better start explaining."

"Why," said the Dog, amazed at my stupidity, "I think it must be perfectly clear exactly what I am. As a competitor of these bowling balls, I must automatically be classified as a friend of yours."

By this time the numbness had worn off enough for me to climb into the car. Somehow I didn't seem to care too much what happened any more. The thought crossed my mind that maybe the Dog was another gang of bowling balls, made up like a dog instead of like a man, but if he was, I was set to take him on at any given moment. I had got over being scared, at least to some extent, and I was getting sore. It was a hell of a world, I told myself, when a man would come unstuck and turn into a bunch of jet-black balls and when a dog waited in a car and struck up a sprightly conversation as soon as one showed up.

I suppose, at that particular time, I didn't quite believe it. But the Dog was there and he was talking to me and there wasn't much that I could do except to go along with it—with the gag, I mean.

"Why don't you," asked the Dog, "give the sack to me? I will hang onto it, I assure you, with the utmost concentration and with the grip of death. I will make it very much my business they do not get away."

So I handed over the sack to him and he reached out a paw and, so help me God, that paw grabbed hold of the sack as neatly as if it had sprouted fingers.

I took the gun out of my pocket and laid it in my lap.

"What kind of instrument is that?" asked the Dog, not missing anything.

"This is a weapon called a gun," I told him, "and with it I can blow a hole clear through you. One wrong move out of you, buster, and I will let you have it."

"I will try my very best," said the Dog quite matter-of-factly, "to make no wrong move at all. I can assure you that I am very much on the side of you in this which is transpiring."

"That is just fine," I said. "See you keep it that way."

I started the car and turned around, heading down the lane.

"I am glad that you were agreeable," said the Dog, "to hand this sack to me. I have had some experience in the handling of these things."

"Perhaps, then," I told him, "you might suggest where we go from here."

"Oh, there are many ways," said the Dog, "of disposing of them. I would venture to suggest, sir, that we should choose a method that is sufficiently restrictive and, perhaps, a little painful."

"I wasn't thinking," I said, "of disposing of them. I went to a lot of trouble to get them in that sack."

"That is too bad," said the Dog regretfully. "Believe me, it is poor policy to let these things survive."

"You keep calling them these things," I pointed out, "and yet you say you know them. Haven't they a name?"

"Name?"

"Yes. Designation. Descriptive term. You have to call them something."

"I get you," said the Dog. "There are times I do not catch so quick. I require a little time."

"And before I forget to ask you, how come you can talk to me? There is no such thing as a talking dog."

"Dog?"

"Yes, the thing you are. You look just like a dog."

"How marvelous!" cried the Dog, enraptured. "So that is what I am. I had met creatures of my general appearance, but they were so different from me and of so many different types. At first I tried communicating with them, but—"

"You mean you're really as you are. You aren't something built out of something else, like our friends there in the sack?"

"I am myself," the Dog said proudly. "I would be nothing else even if I could."

"But you haven't answered how you can talk to me."

"My friend, if you please, let's not go into that. It would require so much explanation and we have so little time, I am, you see, not really talking with you. I am communicating, but—"

"Telepathy?" I asked.

"Come again—and slowly."

I told him what telepathy was, or was supposed to be. I made a bad job of it, principally, I suppose, because I knew very little of it.

"Roughly," said the Dog. "Not exact, however."

I let it go at that. There were other things that were more important.

"You've been hanging around my place," I said. "I saw you yesterday."

"Why, certainly," said the Dog. "You were—let me try to put this right—you were the focal point."

"The focal point," I said, amazed. All this time I had been thinking I'd just fallen into it. Some guys are like that. If lightning hits a tree in a thousand-acre forest, they'll be standing underneath it.

"They knew," said the Dog, "and, of course, I knew. You mean that you were ignorant?"

"You said a mouthful, buster."

We had reached the end of Timber Lane and were out on the highway now, heading back for town.

"You didn't answer me," I said, "when I asked what these things are. The name you have for them. Come to think of it, there are a lot of things you haven't answered."

"You gave me no chance," said the Dog. "You ask me things too fast. And you have a funny thinker. It keeps churning round and round."

The window on his side of the car was open several inches and a sharp breeze was blowing in. It was blowing back his whiskers, smooth against his jaws. They were heavy, ugly jaws, and he kept them closed. They didn't move as if he had been talking—with his mouth, I mean.

"You know about my thinker?" I asked him feebly.

"How else," rejoined the Dog, "could I converse with you? And it's most disorderly and moving very fast. It will not settle down."

I thought that over and decided maybe he was right. Although I didn't like the connotations of what he'd said. I had a sneaking feeling that he might know everything I knew or thought, although, God knows, he didn't act that way.

"To return to your question about the whatness of these things," said the Dog, "we do have a designation for them, but it does not translate into anything I can say to make you understand. Among many other things and in the context in which we here are concerned with them, they are realtors. Although you must realize the term is but approximate and has many qualifications I am helpless to express."

"You mean they sell houses?"

"Oh no," said the Dog, "they would not think to bother with a thing so trivial as a single building."

"With a planet, perhaps?"

"Well, yes," said the Dog, "although it would have to be a most unusual planet, of unusual value. They usually don't concern themselves with anything much less than a solar system. And it has to be a good one or they won't even touch it."

"Now, let us get this straight," I said. "You say they deal in solar systems."

"Your understanding," said the Dog, "leaves nothing to be desired. That is the simple fact alone, however. A complete understanding of the situation would tend to become just a bit complex."

"But who do they buy these solar systems for?"

"Now," said the Dog, "we begin to enter into deepish water. No matter what I told you, you would attempt to equate it with your own economic system, and your economic system—pardon me if I hurt your feelings—is the most outlandish I have ever seen."

"It just happens that I know," I told him, "they're buying up this planet."

"Ah yes," said the Dog, "and most dirty in their dealings, as they always are."

I didn't answer him, for I got to thinking how ridiculous it was that I should be talking to a thing that was a dead ringer for an outsize dog about another race of aliens that were buying up the Earth and doing it, according to my alien friend, in their usual dirty manner.

"You see," the Dog went on, "they can be anything. They never are themselves. Their entire mode of operation is based upon deceit."

"You said they were competitors of yours. Then you must be a realtor yourself."

"Yes, thank you," said the Dog, greatly pleased, "and of the highest class."

"I suppose, then, if these bowling balls, or whatever they may be, had failed to buy the Earth, you'd bought it up yourself."

"No, never," the Dog protested. "It would have been unethical. That is why, you understand, I have interested myself. The present operation will give the entire galactic realty field a exceedingly black eye, and this cannot be allowed to happen. Realty is an ancient and an honorable profession and it must retain its pristine purity."

"Well, that is fine," I said. "I am glad to hear you say it. What do you intend to do?"

"I really do not know. For you work against me. There is no help in you."

"Me?"

"No, not you. Not you alone. All of you, I mean. The silly rules you have."

"But why do they want it? Once they get the Earth, what will they do with it?"

"I see you do not realize," said the Dog, "exactly what you have. There are, I must inform you, few planets such as this one that you call the Earth. It is, you see, a regular dirt-type planet, and planets such as it are few and far between. It is a place where the weary may rest their aching bones and solace their aching eyes with a gentle beauty such as one seldom comes across. There have been built, in certain systems, orbiting constructions which seek to simulate such conditions as occur here naturally. But the artificial can never quite approach the actual, and that is why this planet is so valuable as a playground and resort.

"You realize," he said apologetically, "that I am simplifying and using rough approximations to fit your language and your concepts. It is not, really, as I have told it to you. In many of its facets, it is entirely different. But you gain the main idea, and that is the best that I can do."

"You mean," I asked, "that once these things have the Earth they will run it as a sort of galactic resort?"

"Oh no," said the Dog; "that would be quite beyond them. But they will sell it to those who would. And they'll get a good price for it. There are many pleasure palaces built in space and a lot of simulated Earth-type planets where beings may go for outings and vacations. But, actually, there is really nothing which can substitute for a genuine dirt-type planet. They can get, I may assure you, whatever they may ask."

"And this price they'll ask?"

"Smell. Scent. Odor," said the Dog. "I do not grasp the word."

"Perfume?"

"That is it—perfume. An odor for the pleasure. To them the odor is the thing of beauty. In their natural form it is their greatest, perhaps their only, treasure. For in their natural state they are not as you and I—"

"I have seen them," I told him, "in what I would presume would be their natural state. The ones you have there in the sack."

"Ah, then," said the Dog, "perhaps you understand. They are as lumps of nothing."

He joggled the sack he was holding savagely, bouncing the bowling balls together.

"They are lumps of nothing," he declared, "and they lie there, soaked in their perfume, and that is the height of happiness, if things like this be happy."

I sat there and thought about it and it was outrageous. I wondered for a moment if the Dog might not be kidding me, and then I knew he wasn't. For he, himself, if this were no more than kidding, must then necessarily be a part of the joke. For he was, in his own way, as grotesque and incongruous as the things imprisoned in the sack.

"I am sorry for you," said the Dog, not sounding very sad, "but you have yourself to blame. All these silly rules . . ."

"You said that once before," I told him. "What do you mean—all these silly rules?"

"Why, the ones about each one having things."

"You mean our property laws."

"I suppose that is what you term them."

"But you said the bowling balls would sell the Earth—"

"That's different," said the Dog. "I had to say it your way because there was no way of telling you except in your own way. But I can excellently assure you it is a different way."

And, of course, it would be, I told myself. No two alien cultures, more than likely, ever would arrive at the same way of doing things. The motivations would be different and the methods would be different, because the cultures in themselves could never be parallel. Even as the language—not the words alone, but the concept of the language in itself—could not be parallel.

"This conveyance that you operate," said the Dog, "has intrigued me from the first, and I have had no opportunity to acquaint myself with it. I have been very busy, as you may well imagine, gathering necessary information about many other things."

He sighed. "You have no idea—of course, you haven't; how could you have?—how much there is to learn when one is dropped without preliminary into another culture."

I told him what I knew about the internal-combustion engine and about the drive mechanism which applied the power created by the engine, but I couldn't tell him much. I made a bad job of it, but he seemed to catch the principle involved. I gathered from the way he acted that he had never run across such a thing before. But I gained the distinct impression that he was more impressed by the sheer stupidity of such engineering than by its brilliance.

"I thank you very much," he said, with suavity, "for your lucid explanation. I should not have bothered you with it, but I have the large curiosity. It might have been much better, and somewhat more advantageous, if we had spent the time discussing the disposal of these things."

He joggled the bag of plastic to let me know just what things he meant.

"I know what I am going to do with them," I told him. "We'll take them to a friend of mine by the name of Carleton Stirling. He is a biologist."

"A biologist?" he asked.

"One who studies life," I said. "He can take these things apart and tell us what they are."

"Painfully?" asked the Dog.

"In certain aspects of it, I would imagine so."

"Then it is good," the Dog decided. "This biologist—it seems to me I've heard of other beings that had something similar."

But, from the way he said it, I was fairly certain that he was thinking of something else entirely. There were, I told myself, a lot of ways in which one could study life.

We rode along for a while without saying anything. We were close to the city now and the traffic was beginning to get heavy. The Dog sat rigid in his seat and I could see that the long string of approaching lights had gotten him on edge. Trying to look at them as something I had never seen before, I could realize just how terrifying they might seem to the creature sitting there beside me.

"Let's listen to the radio," I said.

I reached out and turned it on.

"Communicator?" asked the Dog.

I nodded. "Must be almost time for the evening news," I said.

The news had just come on. A violently happy announcer was winding up a commercial about a wonderful detergent.

Then the news reporter said: "A man believed to be Parker Graves, science writer for the *Evening Herald,* was killed just an hour ago by an explosion in the parking lot at the rear of the Wellington Arms. Police believe that a bomb had been placed in his car and exploded when Graves got into it and turned the ignition key. Police are now attempting to make a positive identification of the man, believed to have been Graves, killed in the blast."

Then he went on to something else.

I sat there, startled for a moment, then reached out and turned off the radio.

"What is wrong, my friend?"

"That man who was killed. That was me," I told him.

"How peculiar," said the Dog.

19

I saw the light in his third-floor laboratory and knew Stirling was at work. I pounded on the front door of the building until a wrathful janitor came stumping down the corridor. He motioned for me to leave, but I kept on pounding. Finally he opened the door and I told him who I was. Grudgingly, he let me in. The Dog slipped in beside me.

"Leave the dog outside," ordered the wrathy janitor. "There ain't no dogs allowed."

"That isn't any dog," I said.

"What is it, then?"

"It's a specimen," I told him.

That one stopped him long enough so we could get past him and start up the stairs. Behind us, I could hear him grumbling as he went stumping back down the first-floor corridor.

Stirling was leaning on a lab table, writing in a notebook. He wore a white coat, incredibly dirty.

He looked around at us as we came in and was very casual. He didn't know what time it was. You could see he didn't. He wasn't surprised at our showing up at this unearthly hour.

"Come for the gun?" he asked.

"Brought you something," I said, holding out the sack.

"You have to get that dog out of here," he said. "There are no dogs allowed."

"That isn't any dog," I told him. "I don't know what he calls himself, or where he may have come from, but he is an alien."

Stirling turned all the way around, interested. He squinted at the Dog.

"An alien," he said, not too surprised. "You mean someone from the stars?"

"That," said the Dog, "is exactly what he means."

Stirling crinkled up his brow. He didn't say a word. You could almost hear him thinking.

"It had to happen sometime," he finally said, as if he were delivering an opinion of some weight. "No man could foresee, of course, how it would come about."

"So you're not surprised," I said.

"Oh, of course, surprised. By the form of our visitor's appearance, however, rather than the fact."

"Glad to meet you," said the Dog. "I understand you are a biologist, and that is something I find most interesting."

"But this sack," I told Stirling, "is really why we came."

"Sack? Oh yes, I thought you had a sack."

I held it up so he could see it. "They are aliens, too," I told him.

It was getting damn ridiculous.

He quirked an eyebrow at me.

Quickly, stumbling over my words, I told him what they were, or what I thought they were. I don't know why I had that terrible sense of urgency to get it blurted out. It was almost as if I thought that we had little time and had to get it done. And maybe I was right.

Stirling's face was flushed with excitement now and his eyes had taken on a glitter of dark intensity.

"The very thing," he said, "I talked about this morning."

I grunted questioningly, not remembering.

"A nonenvironmental being," he explained. "Something that can live anywhere, that can be anything. A lifeform that has a letter-perfect adaptability. Able to adjust to any condition—"

"But that's not what you talked about," I told him, for now I remembered what he'd said.

"Well, maybe not," he admitted. "Maybe not exactly what I had in mind. But the result would be the same."

He turned back to the laboratory bench and pulled out a drawer and burrowed into it, thrusting stuff aside. Finally he came up with what he had been after, a transparent plastic bag.

"Here," he said, "let's dump them into this. Then we can have a look at them."

He held the bag, stretching its mouth as wide as he could. With the help of the Dog, I upended the improvised sack and shook the bowling balls out of it into the plastic sack. A few scraps and pieces fell out on the floor. Without bothering to shape themselves into balls, they snaked swiftly for the sink, swarmed up its iron legs, and tumbled down into the basin.

The Dog had started to give chase, but they were too fast for him. He came back crestfallen, his ears drooping and his tail at modified half-mast.

"They retreated down the drain," he told us.

"Oh well," said Stirling, happy and elated, "we have most of them right here."

He tied a good stout knot in the top of the sack and hoisted it up. He passed a hook hanging from a standard above the bench through the knot and the sack hung there, suspended in midair. The plastic was so transparent that you could see the bowling balls without any trouble, every line and shade of them.

"You," the Dog asked anxiously, "intend to take them apart?"

"In time," said Stirling. "First I'll watch them and study them and put them through their paces."

"Tough paces?" the Dog asked anxiously.

"Say, what have we here?" asked Stirling.

"He doesn't like our friends," I said. "They're cutting in on him. They're lousing up his racket."

Off to one side of the room, a telephone purred quietly.

We all stood silent, stricken.

The telephone rang again.

There was something horrifying in the tinkling of the bell. We had been standing there, all snug and all alone, and the bowling balls, for the moment, had been no more than academic objects of great curiosity. But the phone's ring changed all that and the world came crashing in. There now was no aloneness and there was no snugness, for now we were not alone concerned, and the things hanging in the plastic bag were now far from academic: they were now a menace and a threat and something to be feared and hated.

Now I saw the great black of the night outside and could sense the coldness and the arrogance that held the world entrapped. The room contracted to a cold place of gleaming light shattering on the shine of the laboratory bench and the sink and glassware, and I was a feebleness that stood there, and the Dog and Stirling had no more strength than I.

"Hello," said Stirling on the phone. And then he said, "No, hadn't heard it. There must be some mistake. He is here right now."

He listened for a moment and then cut in. "But he's right here with me. He and a talking dog."

"No, he isn't drunk. No, I tell you, he's all right—"

I strode forward. "Hey, give it to me!" I yelled.

He shoved the receiver at me and I could hear Joy's voice: "You, Parker—what is going on? The radio—"

"Yeah, I heard it. Those radio guys are crazy."

"Why didn't you phone me, Parker? You knew that I would hear it—"

"No, how could I know? I was busy. I had a lot of things to do. I found Atwood and he broke up into bowling balls and I caught him in a sack and there was this dog waiting in the car—"

"Parker, are you all right?"

"Sure," I said. "Sure, I am all right."

"Parker, I'm so scared."

"Hell," I said, "there's nothing to be scared of now. It wasn't me in the car, and I found Atwood and—"

"That isn't what I mean. There are things outside."

"There are always things outside," I told her. "There are dogs and cats and squirrels and other people—"

"But there are things that pad. They are all around the place and they are looking in and—please come and get me, Parker!"

She scared me. This wasn't just a foolish woman frightened by the darkness and her own imagination. There was something in her voice, some restrained quality fighting to hold out against hysteria, that convinced me it was not imagination.

"All right," I said. "Hold on. I'll be there as soon as I can make it."

"Parker, please . . ."

"Get on your coat. Stay by the door and watch for the car. But don't come out until I come up the walk to get you."

"All right." She said it almost calmly.

I banged up the phone and swung around to Stirling.

"The rifle," I said.

"Over in the corner."

I saw it leaning there and went to pick it up. Stirling rummaged in a drawer and came up with a box of cartridges and handed them to me. I broke the box and some of the cartridges spilled onto the floor. Stirling bent to pick them up.

I rammed shells into the magazine, dumped the rest of them into my pocket.

"I'm going to get Joy," I told him.

"There's something wrong?" he asked.

"I don't know," I said.

I pounded out the door and down the steps.

The Dog followed at my heels.

20

Joy lived in a small house out in the northwest part of town. For years she had been talking, ever since her mother died, of selling the place and moving into an apartment building closer to the office. But she had never done it. Something held her there—perhaps the old associations and sentimental ties, perhaps the unwillingness to take the chance of moving somewhere else and then not liking it.

I picked a street where I knew the blinking traffic lights would be to my advantage and I made good time.

The Dog, sitting in the seat beside me, with the wind from the partly-open window plastering his whiskers smooth against his face, asked one question only.

"This Joy," he said, "is a good companion?"

"The very best," I told him.

He sat considering that. You could almost hear him considering it. But he said no more.

I cheated on the lights and went faster than the law allowed and wondered all the way what I would tell a cop if one came roaring after me. But none did and I pulled up in front of Joy's house with the brakes full on and the tires whining on the pavement, and the Dog piled up against the windshield quite surprised by it.

The house sat back some distance from the street and was sur-
rounded by an ancient picket fence, which enclosed a yard half
choked with trees and shrubs and zigzag, wandering flower beds.
The front gate stood open, as it had stood ever since I'd known the
place, sagging on its rusty hinges. I saw that the porch light was on
and that there were lights in the front hall and living room.

I jumped out of the car, dragging the rifle with me, and raced
around the car. The Dog beat me to the gate and went tearing
through it, plunging madly into the shrubbery jungle off the brick-
paved walk. I caught one glimpse of him as he disappeared, and his
ears were laid back tight against his skull, his lips were parted in a
snarl, and his tail was at full mast.

I went through the gate and pounded up the walk, while off to
the left, in the direction in which the Dog had gone, there suddenly
erupted a most unholy and bloodcurdling racket.

The front door came open and Joy ran across the porch. I met
her on the steps. She hesitated for a moment, looking off into the
yard from where all the noise was coming.

The racket had grown louder now. It was a hard thing to
describe. It sounded something like a calliope that had gone rav-
ing mad, and intermingled with it was the undertone of something
large running angrily and swiftly through a field of tall, dry grass.

I grabbed Joy's arm and shoved her down the walk.

"Dog!" I shouted. "Dog!"

The racket still kept on.

We reached the sidewalk and I pushed Joy into the front seat
and slammed the door.

There still was no sign of the Dog.

Lights were going on in a few of the houses up and down the
street and I heard a door bang as someone came out on a porch.

I ran back to the gate.

"Dog!" I shouted once again.

He came charging out of the shrubbery, tail tucked tight against
his rump and slobbery foam streaming from his wetted whiskers.

There was something running close behind him—a black and knobby something with the entire front of it a gaping, hungry mouth.

I had no idea what it was. I had no idea what to do.

What I did I did instinctively, without any thought at all.

I used the rifle like a golf club. Why I didn't shoot, I don't know. Perhaps there was no time to; perhaps there was another reason. Perhaps I sensed that a bullet would be useless against the charging maw.

Before I knew what I was about, I had hands around the barrel and the butt was back behind my shoulders and was swinging forward.

The Dog was past me and the knobby shape was coming through the gate and the rifle was a vicious club that almost whistled as it swung. Then it hit and there was no shock. The black thing spattered and the butt went though it—I mean through it, like a knife through butter—and there was a gummy mess running on the sidewalk and the pickets dripped.

There was a floundering in the shrubbery and I knew that there were others coming, but I didn't wait. I turned and ran. I ran around the car and tossed the rifle into the seat alongside Joy, then leaped in myself. I had left the motor running and I gunned the car out from the curb and went up the street with the accelerator tight against the floor.

Joy was huddled in the seat, sobbing softly.

"Cut it out," I told her.

She tried to but she couldn't.

"They always do it short," the Dog said from the back seat. "They always do it half. They do not acquire the intestines to do it as they should."

"You mean the guts," I told him.

Joy stopped her bawling.

"Carleton said you had a talking dog," she said half angrily, half frightened, "and I don't believe it. What kind of trick is this?"

"No trick, my fair one," said the Dog. "Do you not think I enunciate most clearly?"

"Joy," I told her, "drop everything you ever knew. Get rid of all convictions. Forget everything that's right and logical and proper. Imagine yourself in a sort of ogre-land, where anything can happen, and mostly for the worst."

"But—" she said.

"But that's the way it is," I said. "What you knew this morning isn't true tonight. There are talking dogs that aren't really dogs. And there are bowling balls that can be anything they choose. They're buying up the Earth, and Man, perhaps, no longer owns it, and you and I, even now, may be hunted rats."

In the glow of the instrument panel, I could see her face, the puzzle and the wonderment and hurt, and I wanted to put my arms around her and hold her close and try to wipe away some of the puzzlement and hurt. But I couldn't do it. I had a car to drive and I had to try to figure out what we would do next.

"I don't understand," she said, and she kept her voice calm, but there was strain and terror just beneath the calmness. "There was the car . . ."

She reached out a hand and grabbed my arm.

"There was the car," she said.

"Take it easy, gal," I told her. "Take it very easy. All that is behind us. What worries me is what is up ahead."

"You were afraid to go out to the car," she said. "You thought you were a coward. It worried you—that fear. And yet it saved your life."

The Dog said from the back seat: "It might interest you that there is a car behind us."

21

I looked into the rear-vision mirror and the Dog was right. There was a car behind us. It was a one-eyed car.

"Maybe it doesn't mean a thing," I said.

I slowed down and made a left-hand turn. The car behind us also made the turn. I made another left and then a right and so did the other car.

"Might be the police," said Joy.

"With just one light?" I asked. "And if it were they'd have the siren and the red light going the speed we were hitting back there."

I made a few more turns. I got on a boulevard and opened up and the car behind us matched our speed.

"What do we do now?" I asked. "I had intended to go back to the university and up to Stirling's lab. We need to talk with him. But we can't do it now."

"How's the gas?" asked Joy.

"Better than a half a tank."

"The cabin," Joy said.

"You mean Stirling's cabin?"

She nodded. "If we could take his boat and get out in the lake."

"They'd turn into a Loch Ness monster."

"Maybe not. Maybe they have never heard of the Loch Ness monster."

"Then into some other aquatic monster from some other world."

"But we can't stay in the city, Parker. Stay here and the police will get into the act."

"Maybe," I told her, "that would be the best thing that could happen."

But I knew it wasn't. The police would haul us in and we'd lose a lot of time and we could talk from now till doomsday and they'd not believe a word we said about the bowling balls. And I shivered to think of what would happen if they found a talking dog. They'd figure I was a ventriloquist and was playing tricks on them and they'd be really sore.

I switched over a half a dozen blocks or so until I hit a highway leading north and out of town. If I had to head for anywhere, maybe Stirling's cabin was as good as any.

There wasn't any traffic, just a truck every now and then, and I really opened up. The needle hit eighty-five and hung there. I could have pushed it harder, but I was afraid to do it. There were some tricky curves up ahead and I had a hard time remembering exactly where they were.

"Still following?" I asked.

"Still following," said the Dog, "but they have fallen off. They are not so near."

I knew then that we weren't going to shake them. We could build up some distance on them, but they would still be there. Unless they missed us at the turnoff for the cabin they'd come piling in behind us—no more than two or three minutes behind us. And I couldn't be sure we could duck them at the turnoff.

If I was going to shake them, there was going to have to be another way to do it.

The character of the land was changing now. We had left behind us the flat agricultural area and were entering the humpy sand hills covered by evergreens and dotted with small lakes. And it was just beyond, if my memory were not wrong, that the road began to curve—several miles of wicked curves that snaked in and out between the jagged hillocks and the swamps and lakes that lay between them.

"How far are they behind us?" I asked.

"A mile or so," said Joy.

"Listen."

"I am listening."

"I'll stop the car when we hit the curves ahead. I'll get out. You take the wheel. Drive on for a ways, then stop and wait. When you hear me shoot, come back."

"You're crazy," she told me angrily. "You can't tangle with them. You don't know what they'll do."

"We're even, then," I said. "They don't know what I'll do."

"But you alone—"

"Not me alone," I told her. "I have old Betsy there. She'll drop a moose. She'll stop a charging grizzly."

We hit the first of the curve and ground around it. I had hit it too fast and I had to fight the wheel while the tires screamed in shrill protest.

Then we hit the second, still too fast, and finally the third. I put on the brakes, hard, and the car skidded to a halt, half slewed across the road. I grabbed the rifle and, opening the door, slid out.

"All yours," I said to Joy.

She didn't argue or protest. She didn't say a word. She had made her protest and I had brushed it off and that was the end of it. She was an all-right gal.

She slid underneath the wheel. I stepped to one side and the car gunned off. The taillights winked around the curve and I was alone.

The quiet was frightening. There was no sound except the faint rustling of the few remaining leaves in an aspen tree that stood among the pines and the ghostly sighing of the pines themselves. The hills loomed jagged black against the paler sky. And there was the smell of wilderness and the feel of autumn.

The gun felt gummy and I rubbed my hand along it. It was greasy, sticky greasy. And it had a smell—the shaving lotion smell I first had smelled that morning

This morning, I thought—good God, had it only been this morning! I tried to track it back and it was a thousand years ago. It could not have been this morning.

I moved a bit off the road and stood on the shoulder. I rubbed my hand along the rifle stock, trying to rub off the gummy grease. But it would not wipe off. My palm slid over it.

In a few more seconds a car would come around that curve, probably traveling fast. And when I fired, the shooting would be fast and almost by instinct, for I'd be shooting in the dark.

And what, I wondered, if it should turn out to be a regular car, a normal, human car carrying law-abiding humans? What if it were not following us at all, but by some odd happenstance had simply taken the same route that I had taken in attempting to escape it?

I thought about it and the sweat broke out of my armpits and trickled hotly down my ribs.

But it couldn't be, I told myself. I had done a lot of turning and a lot of twisting, and none of that turning and that twisting had made any sense at all. And yet the one-eyed car had followed us on every twist and turn.

The road curved to the top of one of the hillocks, then curled along its side. When the car came around the curve it would be silhouetted for a moment against the paler sky, and it was in that instant that I had to shoot.

I half raised the gun and I found my hands were trembling, and that was the worst thing that could happen. I lowered the gun again and fought to get control, to stop the trembling, but it was no use.

I made another try. I raised the gun again and, even as I did the car came around the curve, and in that single instant I saw the thing that stopped the trembling, that froze me in my tracks and turned me steady as a rock.

I fired and worked the bolt and fired again and worked the bolt once more but did not shoot the third time, for there was no need. The car had left the road and was tumbling down the hillside, crashing through the thickets, banging into trees. And as it rolled the light from the single headlight still miraculously burning, swept across the sky like a probing searchlight.

Then the light was gone and the silence closed in once again. There was no further sound of something crashing own the hill.

I lowered the rifle and released the bolt and eased it back in place with the trigger held.

I let out the breath that I had been holding and took another one, a deep breath.

For it had been no human car; there'd not been humans in it.

When it had come around the curve, in that fleeting second when I could see the outline of it, I had seen that the single fight had been not on either side but positioned directly in the center of the windshield.

22

A car stood in the little yard in front of the cabin as I pulled up before it.

"What is going on?" I asked of no one in particular.

"Is there anyone," asked Joy, "that Carleton would loan the cabin to?"

"Not that I know about," I told her.

I got out and walked around in front of the car.

The wind was swaying the small pine trees and they were talking back. The waves chuckled on the beach and I could hear the *chunk-chunk* sound of Stirling's boat as it pounded gently against the pier.

Joy and the Dog came from the car and stood there beside me. I had kept the engine running, and the headlights bathed the cabin in their fight.

The cabin's door opened and a man came out. Apparently he had dressed hastily, for he was still buckling his belt. He stood and stared at us and then came slowly down the steps off the little porch. He wore pajama tops and he had bed-room slippers on his feet.

We stayed and waited for him and he came toward us hesitantly, across the yard, blinking in the light. He probably was no more than middle-aged, but he looked older. His face was rough with stubble and his uncombed hair stuck out in all directions.

"You folks looking for someone?" he asked.

He stopped about six feet away and peered at us, the light bothering his vision.

"We came up to spend the night," I said. "We didn't know anyone was here."

"You own the cabin, mister?"

"No, a friend of mine."

The man swallowed. I could see him swallow. "We ain't got no right here," he said. "We just moved in because it seemed the thing to do. There was no one using it."

"You just moved in without asking anyone?"

"Look, mister," said the man, "I don't want no trouble. There were other cabins here we could have moved into, but it just so happens that we picked this one. We had no place to go and the missus, she was sick. From worry, mostly, I'd suppose. She never was a hand to be sick before."

"How come no place to go?"

"Lost my job," he said, "and there was no other work and we lost the house. The bank foreclosed on us. And the sheriff threw us out. The sheriff didn't want to, but he had to. The sheriff felt real bad about it."

"The people in the bank?"

"New people," he said. "Some new people came in and bought the bank. The other people, the folks that were there before, they'd not have thrown us out. They would have given us some time."

"And new people bought the place you worked," I said.

He looked at me, surprised. "How did you know that?" he asked.

"It figures," I told him.

"Hardware store," he said. "Just up the road a piece. Up by the all-night service station. Sold sports stuff mostly. Hunting and fishing stuff and bait. Not much of a job. Didn't pay too much, but it made us a living."

I didn't say anything more. I couldn't think of anything to say.

"I'm sorry about the lock," he said. "We had to break the back-door lock. If we could have found a cabin that wasn't locked, we would have used that one. But they all were locked."

"One of the bedroom windows was unlatched," I told him. "It shoves a little hard, but you could have got it up. Stirling always left it that way so friends of his could get in if they wanted to. You had to stand on a chunk of wood or something to reach the window, but you could have gotten in."

"This Stirling? He's the man who owns the place?"

I nodded.

"You tell him we are sorry. Sorry about moving in and busting up the lock. I'll wake the others now and we'll get out right away."

"No," I said. "You stay right where you are. If you had a place where the lady could catch a bit of sleep."

"I'm all right," said Joy. "I can sleep out in the car."

"You'll get cold," said the man. "This time of year it gets right chilly out."

"Some blankets on the floor, then. We'll make out."

"Look," asked the man, "why ain't you sore at me?"

"Friend," I told him, "this isn't any time for anyone to be getting sore at anyone. The time is here when we have to work with one another and take care of one another. We have to hang together."

He peered at me suspiciously, a bit uneasily.

"You a preacher or something of the sort?" he asked me.

"No, I'm not," I said.

I said to Joy: "I want to drive up to the service station and phone Stirling. To tell him we're all right. He might have been expecting us back at the laboratory."

"I'll go back in," said the man, "and figure out a way so you can spend the night. If you want us to get out, we will."

"Not at all," I said.

We got back into the car and I turned around. The man stood watching us.

"What is going on?" asked Joy as we started up the road toward the main highway.

"It's just the beginning," I told her. "There'll be more and more of it. More who lose their jobs and more who lose their homes. Banks bought up to shut off credit. Business places bought and closed to destroy jobs. Houses and apartment buildings purchased and the people evicted and no place for them to go."

"But it's inhuman," she protested.

"Of course, it is inhuman." And, of course, it was. These things weren't human. They didn't care what happened to the human race. The human race was nothing to them, nothing more than a form of life cluttering up a planet that could be used for other things. They would use the humans just as the humans once had used the animals that had cluttered up the land. They'd get rid of them, any way they could. They'd shove them to one side. They'd squeeze them tight together. They'd fix it so they'd die.

I tried to envision how it all would work and it was a hard thing to envision. The basic pattern was there, but the scope was far too large to grasp. To be effective, the scope of the operation must necessarily be worldwide. And if the operation had filtered down to a small-town bank and a crossroads store, then it must mean that, in the United States, at least, the operation—so far as industry, business, and finance were concerned—must be nationwide. For no one would buy up a crossroads business until he had in hand as well the mighty industrial complexes which were the lifeblood of the country. And no one would bother with a small-town bank unless he had the bigger banks under his control as well. For years the bowling balls had been buying stock or taking options on it, had been, more than likely, infiltrating pseudo-humans, such as Atwood, into strategic positions. For they could not afford to move so openly as they now were moving until they had the basic business of the country held within their hands.

And there were places, of course, where the operation wouldn't work. It would be effective only in those nations where private enterprise had flourished, where the people owned the industrial and financial institutions, and where natural resources came under private ownership. It would not work in Russia and it would not work in China, but perhaps it didn't have to. Perhaps it didn't have to work anywhere except in the majority of the great industrial nations. Close down the bulk of the world's industry and shut up the world's financial institutions and the world was whipped. There would be no trade and no flow of currency or credit and the thing that we called civilization would grind to a shuddering halt.

But there was still a question to which there was no answer—a question that bobbed just beneath the surface, popping into view a dozen times a thought: Where had the money come from?

For it would take money, perhaps more money than there was in all the world.

And there was another question just as pertinent: When and how had the money all been paid?

The answer was that it couldn't have been paid. For if it had, the banks would be overflowing with it and the banking systems would be aware that there was something wrong.

Thinking of that, I remembered something that Dow Crane had said just that afternoon. The banks, he had said, were bursting at their seams with money. Overflowing with it. Cash money that people had been bringing in for a week or so.

So maybe it had been paid, or a big part of it. All at once, all engineered so the payments would span no more than a week, all the sales and options and agreements set up in such a fashion that there would have been nothing to disturb the financial picture, to tip off anyone that there was something going on.

And if it had reached that point, I told myself, then mankind's position was impossible, or very close to it.

But even after all the conjecture, all the hinted answers, there was still the question: Where had all the money come from?

THEY WALKED LIKE MEN

Certainly not from anything the bowling balls had brought from their alien planet and had sold on Earth. For if they had sold enough of it, whatever it might be, to get together the working capital they needed, there would have been some sign of it. Unless, of course, it were something of such fantastic value, something, perhaps, that no one had ever thought of as existing—something so valuable that it would appeal to the man who bought certain secret treasures and hugged them close against him, not sharing them, knowing they would decrease in value if he ever dared to share them. Unless it was something like that, it would be impossible to introduce to Earth any trade goods of an alien nature without notice being given them.

"We now communicate," said the Dog, "with the biologist in his laboratory."

"That is right," I told him. "He'll be wondering where we are."

"We must warn him," said the Dog, "to be very careful. I cannot recall if we did or not. Those things in the sack we handed him can be extremely tricky."

"Never fear," I reassured the Dog. "Stirling will take due care. He probably knows more about them now than either of us."

"So we make the call," said Joy, "and then we get some sleep and tomorrow dawns and what do we do then?"

"Damned if I know," I confessed. "We'll think of something. We'll have to think of something. We've got to let the people know what is going on. We'll have to figure out a way to tell them so they will understand and so they will believe."

We reached the main highway, and down ahead of us was the glow of the all-night service station.

I pulled into it and up in front of a pump.

The man came out.

"Fill her up," I said. "You got a pay phone in there?"

He gestured with his thumb. "Right over in the corner, next to the cigarette machine."

I went inside and dialed and fed in the coins when the operator told me to. I heard the buzzing of the signal at the other end.

Someone answered—a gruff, official voice that was not Stirling's voice.

"Who is this?" I asked. "I was calling Carleton Stirling."

The voice didn't tell me. "Who are you?" it asked.

It burned me. Something like that always burns me, but I held my temper and told him who I was.

"Where are you calling from?"

"Now, look—"

"Mr. Graves," the voice said, "this is the police. We want to talk with you."

"Police! What's going on down there?"

"Carleton Stirling's dead. The janitor found him an hour or so ago."

23

I pulled the car up in front of the biology building and got out.

"You better stay here," I told the Dog. "The janitor doesn't like you and I would rather not explain a talking dog to the policeman who is waiting up there."

The Dog sighed gustily, his whiskers blowing out. "I suppose," he said, "it would be somewhat of a shock. Although the now dead biologist took me very calmly. Somewhat better, I might say, than you did yourself."

"He had the advantage of me," I told the Dog. "He had the true scientific outlook."

And I wondered a second later how I could come even close to joking, for Stirling had been my friend and it might well be that I had brought about his death, although at the moment I had no idea of how he might have died.

I remembered him that morning, sprawled upon the chair in the monitoring room with less than another day of life left to him, and how he'd come awake without rancor or surprise and how he'd talked the crazy kind of talk one knowing him had come to expect of him.

"Wait for us," I told the Dog. "We shouldn't be too long."

Joy and I climbed the steps and I was ready to pound upon the door when I found the door to be unlocked. We climbed the stairs and the door to Stirling's lab was open.

Two men were perched upon the lab bench, waiting for us. They had been talking, but when they had heard us coming down the hall they had stopped their talking—we had heard them stop their talking—and sat there waiting for us.

One of them was Joe Newman, the kid who had called me about the bowling balls rolling down the road.

"Hi, Parker," he said, hopping off the bench. "Hi, Joy."

"Hi, yourself," said Joy.

"Meet Bill Liggett," said Joe Newman. "He's from homicide."

"Homicide?" I asked.

"Certainly," said Joe. "They think someone bumped Stirling off."

I swung around to the detective.

He nodded at me. "He was asphyxiated. As if he had been choked. But there wasn't a mark upon him."

"You mean—"

"Look, Graves, if someone strangles a man, he leaves marks on his throat. Bruises, discolorations. It takes a lot of pressure to choke a man to death. Usually there is considerable physical damage."

"And there wasn't?"

"Not a mark," said Liggett.

"Then he could have simply strangled. On something that he ate or drank. Or from muscular contraction."

"The doc says not."

I shook my head. "It doesn't make any kind of sense."

"Maybe it will," said Liggett, "after the autopsy."

"It doesn't seem possible," I said. "I saw him just this evening."

"Far as we can tell," said Liggett, "you were the last man to see him alive. He was alive when you saw him, wasn't he?"

"Very much alive."

"What time?"

"Ten-thirty or so. Maybe close to eleven."

"The janitor said he let you in. You and a dog. He remembers because he told you no dogs were allowed. Says you told him the dog was a specimen. Was he, Graves?"

"Hell, no," I said. "That was just a gag."

"Why did you bring the dog up? The janitor told you not to."

"I wanted to show him to Stirling. We had talked about him. He was a remarkable dog in many ways. He'd been hanging around my apartment building for days and was a friendly dog."

"Stirling like dogs?"

"I don't know. Not especially, I guess."

"Where is this dog now?"

"Down in the car," I said.

"Your car blow up tonight?"

"I don't know," I said. "I heard on the radio it did. They thought that I was in it."

"But you weren't."

"Well, that's apparent, isn't it? You guys find out who it was?"

Liggett nodded. "Young punk who'd been pulled in a couple of times before for stealing cars. Just for the rides. Drive them a few blocks, then leave them."

"Too bad," I said.

"Yeah, isn't it," said Liggett. "You driving a car now?"

"He's driving my car," said Joy.

"You've been with him all evening, lady?"

"We had dinner," Joy said. "I've been with him ever since."

Good gal, I thought. Don't tell this cop a thing. All he'll do is just muck up the situation.

"You waited down in the car while he and the dog came up?"

Joy nodded.

"Seems," said Liggett, "there was a ruckus of some sort out in your neighborhood tonight. You know anything about it?"

"Not a thing," said Joy.

"Don't mind him," said Joe. "He asks a lot of questions. He looks suspicious, too. He has to. That's how he earns a living."

"It does beat hell," said Liggett, "how you two could be mixed up in so many things and still come out so clean."

"It's the way we live," said Joy.

"Why were you up at the lake?" asked Liggett.

"Just for the ride," I said.

"And the dog was with you?"

"Sure, he was. We took him along. He's good company."

The bag was gone from the hook where Stirling had hung it and I couldn't see it anywhere. I couldn't look too hard or Liggett would have noticed.

"You'll have to go down to headquarters," Liggett told me. "The both of you. There are some things we want to get cleared up."

"The Old Man knows about all this," said Joe. "The city desk phoned him about it as soon as you called in to the laboratory."

"Thanks, Joe," I told him. "I imagine we'll be able to take care of ourselves."

Although I wasn't as sure of that as I made it sound. If we went downstairs and the Dog began shooting off his mouth so that Liggett could hear him, there would be hell to pay. And there was the rifle in the car, with its magazine half full and the barrel fouled with powder from the shots I'd taken at the car. I'd have a rough time explaining what I'd been shooting at, even why I carried a rifle in the car at all. And in my pocket was a loaded pistol, and another pocket was loaded down with mixed-up pistol and rifle ammunition. No one—no good citizen—went around in perfect peace and the best intentions with a loaded rifle in his car and a loaded pistol in his pocket.

There was more, too—a whole lot more—that they could trip us up on. There was the phone call Joy had made to Stirling. If the cops really got down to business and in earnest, they'd soon know about that call. And there was every likelihood that whoever had stepped out of his house up in Joy's neighborhood to see about the uproar would have seen the car parked in front of her house and how it had zoomed off down the street, with the accelerator pressed against the floor.

Maybe, I told myself, we should have told Liggett a bit more than we had. Or been a bit more frank in our answers to him. For if he wanted to trip us up, he could trip us up but good.

But if we had, if we'd told him a quarter of the truth, it was a cinch that they'd keep us cooped up for hours down at headquarters while they sneered at the things we told them or tried to rationalize it all into good, solid, modern explanations.

It still might happen, I told myself—all of it might happen— but so long as we could hold it off, we still had a chance that something might pop up that would forestall it.

When I had opened the box of rifle cartridges, some of them had fallen to the floor. Stirling had picked them up. But had he given them to me or had he put them in his pocket or had he laid them on the bench? I tried to remember, but for the life of me I couldn't. If the police had found those cartridges, then they could tie up the rifle in my car with this laboratory, and that would be something else to contribute to their tangle of suspicion.

If there were only time, I thought, I could explain it all. But there wasn't time, and the explanation, in itself, would trigger a rat race of investigation and of questions and of skepticism that would gum up everything. When I came to explain what was going on, it had to be to something other than a room full of police.

There was no hope, I knew, that I could untangle all the mess myself. But I did have to find someone who could. And the police, most emphatically, were not the ones to do it.

I stood there, looking around the laboratory, looking for the bag. But there was something else, just for a moment there was something else. Out of the corner of my eye I caught the motion and the image—the furtive, sneaking sense of motion in the sink, the distinct impression that for an instant an outsize, black angle-worm had thrust a questing head above the edge of the sink and then withdrawn it.

"Well, shall we go?" said Liggett.

"Certainly," I agreed.

I took Joy's arm and she was shivering—not so you could notice, but when I took her arm I could feel the shiver.

"Easy, gal," I said. "The lieutenant here just wants a statement."

"From the both of you," he said.

"And from the dog?" I asked.

He was sore. I could see that he was sore. I should have kept my mouth shut.

We started for the door. When we got to it, Joe said "You're sure, Parker, there's nothing you want me to tell the Old Man?"

I swung around to face him and the lieutenant. I smiled at both of them.

"Not a thing," I said.

Then we went out the door, with Joe following us and the detective following him. The detective closed the door and I heard the latch snap shut.

"You two can drive downtown," said Liggett. "To headquarters. I'll follow in my car."

"Thanks," I said.

We went down the stairs and out through the front door and down the steps to the sidewalk.

"The Dog," Joy whispered to me.

"I'll shut him up," I said.

I had to. For a time he could be no more than a happy, bumbling dog. Things were bad enough without him shooting off his face.

But we needn't have worried.

The back seat was empty. There was no sign of the Dog.

24

The lieutenant escorted us to a room not much larger than a cubbyhole and left us there.

"Be back in just a minute," he said.

The room had a small table and a few uncomfortable chairs. It was colorless and chilly and it had a dark, dank smell to it.

Joy looked at me and I could see that she was scared but doing a good job of trying not to be.

"Now what?" she asked.

"I don't know," I told her. Then I said: "I'm sorry I got you into this."

"But we've done nothing wrong," she said.

And that was the hell of it. We had done nothing wrong and yet here we were, into it clear up to our necks, and with valid explanations for everything that had happened, but explanations that no one would believe.

"I could use a drink," said Joy.

I could have, too, but I didn't say so.

We sat there and the seconds dragged their feet and there was nothing we could say and it was miserable.

I sat hunched in a chair and thought about Carleton Stirling and what a swell guy he had been and how I would miss dropping in on him over at the lab and watching him work and listening to him talk.

Joy must have been thinking about the same thing, for she asked: "Do you think that someone killed him?"

"Not someone," I said. "Something."

For I was positive that it had been the thing or things I'd carried to him in the sheet of plastic that had done him in. I had walked into the laboratory, carrying death for one of my best friends.

"You're blaming yourself," said Joy. "Don't blame yourself. There was no way you could know."

And, of course, there wasn't, but that didn't help too much.

The door opened and the Old Man walked in. There was no one with him.

"Come along," he said. "It's all straightened out. No one wants to see you."

We got up and walked over to the door.

I looked at him, a little puzzled.

He laughed, a short, chuckling laugh. "I pulled no strings," he said. "Not a mite of influence. I flung no weight around."

"Well, then?"

"The medical examiner," he said. "The verdict's heart attack."

"There was nothing wrong with Stirling's heart," I said.

"Well, there was nothing else. And they had to put down something."

"Let's go someplace else," said Joy. "This place gets me down."

"Come up to the office," the Old Man said to me, "and get outside a drink. There is a thing or two I want to talk with you about You want to come along, Joy, or are you anxious to get home?"

Joy shivered. "I'll come along," she said.

I knew what was the trouble. She didn't want to go back to that house and hear things in the yard—hear them prowling there even if there weren't any.

"You take Joy," I said to the Old Man. "I will drive her car."

We went outside and we didn't talk too much. I expected the Old Man would ask me about my car blowing up and perhaps a lot of other things, but he barely said a word.

He didn't even say a great deal in the elevator going up to his office. When we got into the office he went to the liquor cabinet and got out the makings.

"Scotch for you, Parker," he remembered. "How about you, Joy?"

"The same for me," she said.

He fixed the drinks and handed them to us. But he didn't go back of his desk and sit down. Instead he sat down on one of the other chairs with us. Probably he was trying to let us know that he was not the boss but just another member of the staff. There were times when he went to ridiculous lengths to point out his humility, and there were other times, of course, when he had no humility at all.

He had something that he wanted to talk with me about, but he was having trouble getting around to it. I didn't help him any. I sat there, working on the drink, and let him go about it the best way that he could. I wondered just how much he knew or whether he had the slightest idea of what was going on.

And suddenly I knew that the verdict had not necessarily been heart attack and that the Old Man had swung a lot of weight, and the reason that he'd gone to bat for us was because he knew, or thought, I had something and that maybe it was big enough for him to save my neck.

"Quite a day," he said.

I agreed it had been.

He said something about the stupidity of police and I made agreeing noises.

Finally he got around to it. "Parker," he said, "you have got your hooks into something big."

"Could be," I told him. "I don't know what it is."

"Big enough, maybe, for someone to try to kill you."

"Someone did," I said.

"You can come clean with me," he told me. "If it's something that has to be kept under cover, I can help you keep it there."

"This is something I can't tell you yet," I said. "For if I did, you'd think that I was crazy. You wouldn't believe a word of it. It's something I have to have more proof on before I can tell anyone."

He made his face go startled. "As big as that," he said.

"That big," I agreed.

I wanted to tell him. I wanted to talk to someone about it. I wanted to share the worry and the terror of it, but with someone who was willing to believe it and who would be equally as willing to have at least a try at doing something that could be effective.

"Boss," I said, "can you suspend all disbelief? Can you tell me that you'd be ready to at least accept as possible anything I told you?"

"Try me," he said.

"Damn it, that's not good enough."

"Well, all right, then, I will."

"What if I should tell you that aliens from some distant star are here on J3arth and are buying up the Earth?"

His voice turned cold. He thought I was kidding him.

He said: "I'd say that you were crazy."

I got up and put the glass down on the desk top.

"I was afraid of that," I said. "It's what I had expected."

Joy had risen, too. "Come on, Parker," she said. "There's no use staying here."

The Old Man yelled at me: "But, Parker, that's not it. You were kidding me."

"The hell I was," I said.

We went out the door and down the corridor. I thought that maybe he'd come to the door and call us back, but he didn't. I caught a glimpse of him as we turned to go down the stairs, not waiting for the elevator, and he still was sitting in his chair, staring after us, as if he were trying to decide whether to be sore at us, or whether it might not be best to fire us, or whether, after all, there might have been something in the thing I'd told him. He looked small and far away. It was as if I were looking at him through binoculars turned the wrong way around.

We went down three flights of stairs to reach the lobby. I don't know why we didn't take the elevator. Neither of us, apparently, even thought about it. Maybe we just wanted to get out of there the quickest way there was.

We went outside and it was raining. Not much of a rain, just the beginning of a rain, cold and miserable.

We walked over to the car and stood beside it, not getting in just yet, standing there undecided and confused, not knowing what to do.

I was thinking of what had been in the closet back in the apartment (not that I actually knew what had been in there) and what had happened to the car out in the parking lot. I knew that Joy must be thinking about the things that had prowled around the house and might still be prowling there—that, whether they were or not, would keep on prowling from this time forward in her imagination.

She moved over closer and stood tight against me and I put an arm around her, without saying anything, there in the rainy dark, and held her even closer, thinking how we were like two lost and frightened children, huddling in the rain. And afraid of the dark. For the first time in our lives, afraid of the dark.

"Look, Parker," said Joy.

She was holding out a hand, with the palm cupped upward, and there was something in the palm, something she had been carrying in a tight-clenched fist.

I bent to look at it, and in the faint light cast by the streetlamp at the end of the block I saw it was a key.

"It was sticking in the lock on Carleton's laboratory door," she said. "I slipped it out when no one was looking. That stupid detective closed the door without ever thinking of the key. He was so sore at you that he never thought about it. You asking him if he wanted a statement from the dog."

"Good work," I said, and caught her face between my hands and kissed her. Although, even now, I can't imagine why I was so elated at finding we had the laboratory key. It was simply, I guess, that it was a final outwitting of authority, that in a rather grim and terrible game we had won a trick.

"Let's have a look," she said.

I opened the door and ushered her into the car, then walked around it and got in on the other side. I found the key and thrust it in the lock and turned it to start the motor, and even as the engine coughed and caught I tried to jerk it from the lock, realizing even as I did that it was too late.

But nothing happened. The motor purred and there was nothing wrong. There had been no bomb.

I sat there, sweating.

"What's the matter, Parker?"

"Nothing," I said. I put the machine in gear and moved out from the curb. And I remembered those other times I had started up the car, out at the Belmont house, in front of the biology building (twice on that one), again in front of the police station, never thinking of the danger—so maybe it was safe. Maybe the bowling balls never tried something a second time if it failed the first.

I swung into a side street to cut over to University Avenue.

"Maybe it's a wild-goose chase," said Joy. "Maybe the front door will be locked."

"It wasn't when we left," I said.

"But the janitor might have locked it."

He hadn't, though.

We went through the door and climbed the stairs as quietly as we could.

We came to Stirling's door and Joy handed me the key. I fumbled a little but finally got the key inserted and turned it, pushing the door open.

We walked inside and I closed the door, listening to the latch click shut.

A tiny flame burned on the laboratory bench—a small alcohol lamp that I was sure had not been lit before. And beside the bench, perched upon a stool, was a strangely twisted figure.

"Good evening, friends," he said. There was no mistaking the clear, cultivated intonations of that voice.

It was Atwood sitting on the stool.

25

We stood and stared at him and he tittered at us. He probably meant it to be a chuckle, but it came out as a titter.

"If I look a little strange," he told us, "it's because not all of me is here. Some of me got home."

Now that we could see him better, our eyes becoming accustomed to the feeble light, it was apparent that he was twisted and lopsided and that he was somewhat smaller than a man should be. One arm was shorter than the other and his body was far too thin and his face was twisted out of shape. And yet his clothing fit him, as if it had been tailored to fit his twisted shape.

"And another thing," I said. "You haven't got your model."

I fished around in my topcoat pocket and found the tiny doll I'd picked up off the floor of the basement room in the Belmont house.

"Far be it from me," I said, "to make it tough on you."

I tossed the doll toward him and he lifted the shortened arm and, despite the feeble light, caught it unerringly. And as he caught it, during that second when it touched his fingers, it melted into him—as if his body, or his hand, had been a mouth that had sucked it in.

His face became symmetrical and his arms became the same length and the lopsided quality went entirely out of him. But his clothing was a bad fit now and the short sleeve of his jacket was halfway up his arm. He still was smaller, much smaller than I had remembered him.

"Thanks," he said. "It helps One doesn't have to concentrate so hard to hold his shape."

The sleeve was growing down his arm; you could see it grow. And the rest of his clothes were changing, too, so that they would fit him.

"The clothes are a bother, though," he said conversationally.

"That's why you had racks of them in the downtown office."

He looked a little startled; then he said: "Yes, you were there, of course. It had slipped my mind. I must say, Mr. Graves, that you surely get around."

"It's my business," I told him.

"And the other with you?"

"I am sorry," I Said. "I should have introduced you. Miss Kane, Mr. Atwood."

Atwood stared at her. "If you don't mind my saying so," he said, "it occurs to me that you people have the damnedest reproductive setup I have ever seen."

"We like it," Joy said.

"But so cumbersome," he said. "Or, rather, made so cumbersome and so intricate by the social customs and the concepts of morality you have woven round it. I suppose that otherwise it is perfectly all right."

I said: "You wouldn't know, of course."

"Mr. Graves," he said, "you must understand that while we ape your bodies, we need not necessarily subscribe to all the activity connected with those bodies."

"Our bodies," I said, "and perhaps some other things. Like bombs placed in a car.

"Oh yes," he said. "Such simple things as that."

"And traps set before a door?"

"Another simple thing. Not intricate, you know. Complex things are very much beyond us."

"But why the trap?" I asked him. "You tipped your hand on that one. I didn't know about you. I didn't even dream there were such things as you. If there had been no trap—"

"You'd still have known," he said. "You were the one who could have put two and two together. You see, we knew about you. We knew you, perhaps, a good deal better than you knew yourself. We knew what you could do, what you most probably would do. And we know, as well, a little of the happenings immediately ahead. Sometimes we do, not always. There are certain factors—"

"Now wait," I said, "just a goddamn minute. You mean you knew about me. Not just me alone, of course?"

"Certainly not just you alone. But something of every one of you who might at some time be placed in such a position as to become aware of us. Like newsmen and officers of the law and certain public officials and key industrialists and—"

"You studied all of these?"

He almost smirked at us. "Every one of them," he said.

"And there were others than myself?"

"Oh, of course, there were. Quite a number of them."

"And there were traps and bombs—"

"A wide variety of things," he told me.

"You murdered them," I said.

"If you insist. But I must remind you not to be self-righteous. When you came in here tonight you had full intention to pour some acid down the sink."

"Of course," I said, "but now I realize it would have done no good."

"Just possibly," said Atwood, "it would have gotten rid of me—or, at least, the major part of me. I was down that drain, you know."

"Rid of you," I said. "But not of all the others."

"What do you mean?" he asked.

"Get rid of you and there could be another Atwood. Any time you want, there could be another Atwood. Frankly, there's no point to interminably getting rid of Atwoods when there's always, if necessary, another one on tap."

"I do not know," said Atwood thoughtfully. "I can't figure you folks out. There is an undefinable something about you that makes no sense at all. You set up your rules of conduct and you fabricate your neat little social patterns, but you have no patterns of yourselves. You can be incredibly stupid one moment and incredibly brilliant the next. And the most vicious thing about you—the most awful thing about you—is your unspoken, ingrained faith in destiny. Your destiny, not someone else's. It's an appalling quality to even think about."

"And you," I said. "You'd have borne me no ill will if I had poured the acid."

"Not particularly," said Atwood.

"There," I told him, "is a point of difference between us that you should possibly consider. I bear you—or your kind—considerable ill will for your attempts to kill me. And I bear you as much or more, ill will for the murder of my friend."

"Prove it," said Atwood defiantly.

"What's that?"

"Prove I killed your friend. I believe," he said, "that is the proper human attitude. You get away with anything if no one proves you did it. And, likewise, Mr. Graves, you may be confusing viewpoints. Conditions modify them."

"Meaning that in certain other places murder is no crime."

"That," said Atwood, "is the point exactly."

The flame of the alcohol lamp flickered fitfully and set up fleeing shadows that raced around the room. And it was so ordinary, so commonplace, I thought, that we should be here, two products of different planets and of different cultures, talking as if we might have been two men. Perhaps this were so because this other thing, whatever it might be, had assumed the shape of man and had schooled itself in human speech and action and, perhaps, to some extent as well in the human viewpoint. I wondered if the same condition would exist if it were one of the bowling balls, unshaped to human or to any other form, which rested on the stool and talked to us, perhaps as the Dog talked, without the human movement of a mouth. Or if the thing which had become at least a momentary Atwood could talk so easily and well if it had not absorbed so great a knowledge, despite the fact that knowledge might be no more than superficial, of the ways of Earth and Man.

How long, I wondered, had these aliens been upon the Earth and how many of them? For years, perhaps, patiently working themselves into not only the knowledge but the feel of Earth and Man, studying the social patterns and the economic systems and the financial setup. It would take a long time, I realized, because they would not only be starting cold on the bare knowledge in itself but probably would be facing not only an unfamiliar but probably an unknown factor in our maze of property laws and our legal and our business systems.

Joy put her hand on my arm. "Let's leave," she said. "I don't like this character."

"Miss Kane," said Atwood, "we are quite prepared to accept your dislike of us. To tell you the truth, we simply do not care."

"I talked to a family this morning that was worried sick," said Joy, "because they had no place to go. And this evening I saw another family that had been evicted from its home because the father had lost his job."

"Things like that," said Atwood, "have been going on through all your history. Don't challenge me on that. I have read your history. This is no new condition we've created. It is a very old one in your human terms. And we have done it honestly and, believe me, with all due attention to legality.

It was almost, I thought, as if we, the three of us, were acting out an old morality play, with the basic sins of mankind enlarged a millionfold to prove a point by exaggeration.

I felt Joy's grip tighten on my arm and knew that this was perhaps the first time she had realized the true amorality of the creature that we faced. And perhaps, as well, a realization that this creature, this Atwood, was no more than a visual projection of a great, vast horde of others, of an alien force which intended to take the Earth from us. Behind the thing that sat upon the stool one could almost see the ravening blackness which had come from some far star to put an end to Man. And, worse than that, not to Man alone, but to all his works and all his precious dreams, imperfect as all those dreams might be.

The great tragedy, I realized, was not the end of Man himself but the end of all that Man had stood for, all that Man had built and all that he had planned.

"Despite the fact," said Atwood, "that the human race may resent us and, perhaps, even hate us, there is nothing that's illegal, even in your own concept of right and wrong, in anything we've done. There is nothing in the law which restricts anyone, even aliens, from acquiring or from holding property. You, yourself, my friend, or the lady with you, have a perfect right to buy all the property you wish. To purchase and to hold, if that should be your aim, all the property that exists in the entire world."

"Two things would," I said. "One of them is the lack of money."

"And the other?"

"It would be damn poor taste," I told him. "It simply isn't done. And, also, a possible third thing. Something that is called an anti-trust law."

"Oh, those," said Atwood. "We are well aware of them; we have taken certain measures."

"I am sure you have."

"When you get right down," said Atwood, "to the nub of it, the only qualification one needs to do what we have done is to have the money."

"You talk as if money is a new idea to you," I said, for the way he'd said it, that was the way it sounded. "Could it be that money is unheard of elsewhere than Earth?"

"Don't be ridiculous," said Atwood. "There is commerce of a sort, and there are mediums of exchange. Mediums of exchange, but not money possibly as you know it here. Money here on Earth is more than the paper or the metal that you use for money, more than the rows of figures that account for money. Here on Earth you have given money a symbolism such as no medium of exchange has anywhere else that I have ever known or heard of. You have made it a power and a virtue and you have made the lack of it despicable and somehow even criminal. You measure men by money and you calibrate success with money and you almost worship money."

He would have gone on if I'd let him. He was all ready to preach a full-scale sermon. But I didn't let him.

"Look at this business practically," I said. "You're going to lay out, before you're through with it, more cash than the Earth has cost you, much more than it's worth. You'll throw people out of jobs and drive them from their homes and someone will have to try at least to take care of them. Every government on Earth will establish great relief programs and set up doles to help their people, and taxes will go up to pay for all of this. Taxes, mind you, levied on the very property you've bought. You throw the people out of work, you take their homes from them—OK, so you'll take care of them, you'll have to pay the taxes to take care of them."

"I see," said Atwood, mocking, "that your heart bleeds for us, and it's very human of you and I thank you for it. But you need not bother. We'll pay the taxes. We'll very gladly pay them."

"You could overthrow the governments," I said, "and then there'd be no taxes. Perhaps you've thought of that."

"Of course not," said Atwood firmly. "That is something we would not think of doing. That would be illegal. We do not, my friend, overstep the law."

And it was no good, I knew. There was nothing any good.

For the aliens would control the land and the natural resources and all the things that were built upon the land, and they would not use the land in its proper usage—or anything else in the proper way. They would plow no furrow and they would grow no crop. No factory wheel would turn. No metal would be mined. No timber would be cut.

The people would be dispossessed, not alone of their property, but of their heritage. Gone with the land and houses, with the factory and the job, with the retail store and the merchandise, would be the hope and the aspiration and the opportunity—and perhaps the faith—that shaped humanity. It did not matter greatly how much of the property of Earth the aliens actually bought. They need not buy it all. All that, would be necessary would be to stop the wheels of industry, to halt the flow of commerce, to destroy the effectiveness of the financial structure. When that had been done, there'd be an end to jobs and an end to credit and an end to business. And the human dream was dead.

It did not really matter that the aliens buy the homes or the apartment houses, for if all the rest were done, then the four walls that a man called home would be just a place in which to die. Either the purchasing of the homes was a pure campaign of terror or, equally as likely, an indication that the aliens even now did not understand how little they would really have to do to strike the fatal blow.

There would be doles, of course, or some sort of relief program, to keep food in the people's mouths and, where possible, a roof above their heads. And there'd be no lack of money for the doles, for the taxes would be paid most cheerfully by this alien tribe. But in a situation such as this, money would be the cheapest thing there was, and the least effective. What the price of a potato or a loaf of bread when we had reached the last potato and there was no flour for bread?

There would be fighting back, once the situation should be known. Fighting back, not only by the people, but by the governments as well. But by that time the aliens undoubtedly would have set up some sort of defense, perhaps of a kind and nature no one now could guess. Perhaps it would be a scorched-earth defense, with the factories and the homes and all the rest of it going up in flames

or otherwise destroyed so that Man could not regain the things with
which he'd forged a livelihood. There would then be only the land
to fight for, and the bare land in itself would not be enough.

If something could be done immediately, I knew, there was
every chance that, even now, the aliens could be beaten. But to do
anything soon enough required a willingness to believe in what was
going on. And there was no one who'd believe. Bitterly, I realized
that acceptance of the situation in its full and brutal force would
have to wait until the world had been plunged in chaos, and by that
time it well could be too late.

And, standing there, I knew that I was licked and that the world
was licked.

Wells had written, long ago, of aliens who had invaded Earth.
And many, after him, had written other imaginary versions of alien
invasions. But not a one of them, I thought, not a single one, had
come even close to what had really happened. Not one had foreseen
how it could be done, how the very system which we had con-
structed so painfully through the ages should now be turned against
us—how freedom and the right of property had turned out to be a
trap we'd set to catch ourselves.

Joy pulled at my arm. "Leave us go," she said.

I turned with her and headed for the door.

Behind me I heard Atwood chuckling.

"Come see me tomorrow," he said. "You and I maybe can do
business."

26

Outside it was raining more heavily than ever. Not a downpour, but a steady drip that was discouraging. There was a definite edge of chill in the air. It was the kind of night, I thought, for the world we knew to come crashing down. No, not crashing down, for that was too dramatic. Sagging, rather. The kind of a night for the world to come sagging down, weakened without knowing it was being weakened or what had weakened it, and falling so smoothly and so steadily it did not know that it was falling until it had collapsed.

I opened the door of the car for Joy, then slammed it shut again before she could get in.

"I forgot," I said. "There could be a bomb in there."

She looked at me and raised a hand to push away a lock of hair that had blown across her eyes.

"No," she said. "He wants to talk with you. Tomorrow."

"That was just talk," I said. "His way of being funny."

"And even if there is a bomb in there, I'm not walking back to town. Not at this hour and in this rain. And there wasn't one before."

"Let me get in and start it. You stand off—"

"No," she said emphatically. She reached out and jerked the door open.

I walked around the car and got in. I turned the key and the engine started.

"See," she said.

"There could have been," I told her.

"Even if there were, we can't live in continual fear of it," she said. "There are a million ways that they can kill us if that is what they want."

"They killed Stirling. There probably are others they have killed. They made two tries at me."

"And failed each time," she said. "I have a feeling they'll not try again."

"Intuition?"

"Parker, they may have intuition, too."

"What has that to do with it?"

"Maybe nothing," she said. "It's not really what I meant to say. What I meant was that no matter how much they learn about us, how much they try to be like us to carry out their project, they can never learn to think like us."

"So you believe they'll give up if they don't kill someone in two tries."

"Well, not that exactly, although maybe so. But they won't try the same thing twice."

"So I am safe from traps and bombs and something in the closet."

"It may be a superstition with them," she said. "It may be a way of thinking. It may be a logic we don't even know."

She had been thinking about it all the time, I knew. Trying to get it figured out. That pretty little head had been filled with speculation, and the few facts, or quasi facts, that we had in our possession had gone round and round. But there was no way, I thought, to get it figured out. Because you didn't know enough. You were thinking as a human thought and trying to think as an alien thought without knowing how he thought. And even if you did know, there was no guarantee that you could twist the human thought processes into an alien channel.

Joy had put it the other way around. The aliens, she had said, no matter how much they wanted, could never think like us. But they had a better chance to think like us than we to think like them. They had studied us, how long no one could know. And there had been many of them; no one knew how many. Or was that the correct way to say it? Might there not be no more than a single one of them, with that one fractionated into units the size of bowling balls, so that a single one of them could be in many places and be many things at once?

Even if they were individuals, if each bowling ball were a complete and single thing, they still were closer to one another than it was possible for human beings to be close to one another. For it took many of them to make a thing like Atwood or like the girl who'd sat beside me at the bar: it took a lot of them to shape themselves into the simulation of a human being. And in doing that, in taking human form, or any other form, they then must work as one; then must, in very fact, the many become as one.

We rolled down the last of the campus streets and came out on a deserted University Avenue and I headed back for town.

"Now what?" I asked.

"I can't go home," said Joy. "Not back to the house. They might still be there."

I nodded, knowing how it was. And I wondered what the things that had prowled the yard might be. Perhaps some ferocious beast, or, rather, the simulation of some ferocious beast from some other planet. Perhaps many kinds of ferocious beasts from many other planets. Perhaps a great menagerie of terrible life-forms, meant, perhaps, to terrify rather than to harm. No more than bait, perhaps, to pull the three of us together—Joy, the Dog, and I—to get us in one spot. But if they had meant to kill the three of us, then it had been another plan that had failed.

The Dog had said something about the bowling balls' never going far enough, never pushing hard enough, dealing in half measures. I tried to remember what he actually had said, but my memory was hazy. Too much had happened.

And I wondered, too, where the Dog had gone.

"Parker," Joy said, "we have to get some rest. We have to get in out of the rain and get a few hours' sleep."

"Yeah," I said. "I know. My place—"

"I didn't mean your place. It's as bad as mine. We could find a motel, maybe."

"Joy, I have only a dollar or two in my pocket. I forgot to pick up my check."

"I cashed mine," she said. "I have some money, Parker."

"Joy . . ."

"Yes, I know. Don't worry. It's all right."

We drove on down the street.

"What time is it?" I asked.

She held her wrist down so that the light from the dash shone on her watch.

"It's almost four," she told me.

"Quite a night," I said.

She leaned back wearily against the seat, turned her head to look at me.

"Wasn't it," she said. "One car blown up and some poor kid with it, but, thank the Lord, not you; one friend killed without a mark upon him by something from another world; one gal's reputation gone to hell because she is so sleepy she's willing to shack up—"

"Just keep quiet," I said.

I turned off the avenue.

"Where you going, Parker?"

"Back to the office. I have to make a call. Long distance. Might as well let the paper pay for it."

"Washington?" she asked.

I nodded. "Senator Roger Hill. It's time to talk to Rog."

"At this hour of the morning?"

"At any time of day. He's a public servant, isn't he? That's what he tells the people. Around election time. And the country—the whole damn country—needs a public servant now."

"He won't love you for it."

"I don't expect him to."

I pulled the car up to the curb across from the darkened building. There was a faint light from the third floor and a dim glow from the first-floor pressroom.

"Do you want to come with me?"

"No," she said, "I'll stay. I'll lock the doors and wait. I'll watch that no one bombs the car."

27

The office was deserted and had that cold, expectant air that newspaper offices take on when there's no one there. There were janitors, of course, but I saw none of them, and Lightning, the dog-trick office boy, should have been on duty, too, but he, more than likely, was off on some mysterious unofficial errand of his own or had found some corner where he could snatch an hour or two of sleep.

A few lights were burning, but they did no more than add to the ghostly shadow of the place, like distant streetlamps shining on a foggy boulevard.

I went to my desk and sat down in my chair and put out my hand to pick up the phone, but I didn't lift it right away. I sat there, quiet and listening, but for the life of me I didn't know what I was listening to, although it may have been the silence. The room was quiet. There wasn't a whisper of a sound. And it seemed to me that, at this moment, the world was quiet as well—that the silence of this place stretched out beyond these walls to envelop the entire planet and that all the Earth was hushed.

Slowly I lifted the receiver and dialed the operator. She came on in a sleepy voice. There was a bit of polite surprise when I told her who I wanted, as if she, too, was of a mind to rebuke me for calling so great a man as a senator at this time of night But her training kept her from doing it and she told me she would call me back.

I replaced the receiver in its cradle and leaned back in the chair and tried to do some thinking, but the hours were catching up with me and my brain refused to think. For the first time I realized just how tired I was.

I sat there in a fog, with the few lights shining like distant streetlamps and with not a sound around me. And, maybe, said my foggy mind that had refused to think, this is the way the Earth is on this night—a silent planet sitting, tired and beaten, in the silence of not-caring, a planet going to its doom and no one to give a damn.

The phone rang.

"We have your party, Mr. Graves," said the operator.

"Hello, Rog," I said.

"This you, Parker?" said the distant voice. "What the hell's the matter with you at this time of night?"

"Rog," I said, "it's important. You know I wouldn't call you if it were not important."

"I should hope it is. I just got to sleep a couple of hours ago."

"Something keeping you up, Senator?"

"A little get-together. Some of us were talking over several matters."

"Someone worried, Rog?"

"Worried over what?" he asked, as smooth and slick as ice.

"Too much money in the banks, for one thing."

"Look, Parker," he said, "if you're trying to worm something out of me, it's a waste of time."

"Not to worm something out of you. To tell you something. If you'll just listen, I can tell you what is going on. It's a little hard to tell, but I want you to believe me."

"I am listening."

"There are aliens here on Earth," I told him. "Creatures from the stars. I've seen them and I've talked with them and—"

"Now I get it," said the senator. "It's Friday night and you have hung one on."

"You're wrong," I protested. "I'm sober as—"

"You picked up your check and you went out and—"

"But I didn't pick up my check. I was too busy and forgot it."

"Now I know you're drunk. You never miss a check. You are there, standing in line, with your hand out—"

"Goddamn it, Rog, just listen to me."

"Get back to bed," said the senator, "and sleep it off. Then, if you still want to talk to me, call me in the morning."

"To hell with you," I yelled, but he didn't hear me. He already had hung up. The line buzzed dead and empty.

I felt like slamming the receiver down, but I didn't slam it. Something kept me from slamming it, perhaps a deep sense of defeat that chewed away the anger.

I sat there, gripping the receiver in my hand, with the far-off, mosquito buzzing of the empty line, and knew there was no hope— that no one would believe me, that no one would listen to what I had to tell. Almost, I told myself, as if all of them were Atwoods, as if every single one of them was a simulated human, built out of the alien stuff that had invaded Earth.

Come to think of it, I told myself, it wasn't so damn funny. It was something that could happen. It would be exactly the kind of thing the aliens would have done.

Icy insect feet went walking up my spine and I sat there, clutching the receiver, the loneliest human being on the entire Earth.

For I might, I thought, be in truth alone.

What if Senator Roger Hill were not a man, not the same man he had been, say, five years ago? What if what remained of the body of the real, the authentic, the human Roger Hill lay in some hidden place and the bogus, the alien Roger Hill were the man who had just talked with me? What if the Old Man were not the real Old Man at all, but a hideous thing which walked in Old Man form? What if the chairman of some great steel company were no longer human? What if keyman after keyman had been done away with and their places had been taken by something from another world, so formed, so briefed, so perfect that all of them were accepted by their own associates and by their families?

What if the woman who waited in the car outside were not . . .

But that, I told myself, was crazy. That was ridiculous. That could be nothing more than the frustrated fantasy of a mind too worn out, too sick, too shocked to think the way it should think.

I put the receiver back into its cradle and pushed the phone away. I got slowly to my feet and stood shivering in the emptiness and silence.

Then I went downstairs and out into the street, where Joy waited for me.

28

The "No Vacancy" sign was flashing, throwing green and red shadows across the black slick of wet street. On and on it flashed, a warning to the world. And back of it loomed the dark huddle of the units, each with its tiny light above the door and with the soft, fleeting gleam of parked cars picking up the flashing sign.

"No room in the inn," said Joy. "It makes you feel unwanted."

I nodded. It was the fifth motel that we had passed where there was no vacancy. The sign had not always been a flashing sign, but it had been there, glowing in the night. And the flashing of the sign carried no meaning greater than the others, but it was more emphatic and aggressive. As if it were spelling out in grim and final detail that there was no lodging.

Five motels with the forbidding signs and one with no sign at all, but dark and closed and untenanted—a place shut against the world.

I slowed the car and we crunched to a sliding halt. We sat, looking at the sign.

"We should have known," said Joy. "We should have realized. All those people who can't find a place to live. They're ahead of us. Maybe some of them for weeks."

The rain still was sifting down. The windshield wipers whined.

"Maybe it was a bad idea," I told her. "Maybe . . ."

"No," said Joy. "Neither of our places. Parker, I would die."

We drove on. Two more motel signs announced no vacancies.

"It's impossible," said Joy. "There isn't any place. The hotels would be as bad."

"There just might be," I said. "There might be a place. That motel back there. The one that had no sign. The one that was closed up."

"But it was dark. There was no one there."

"There is shelter there," I told her. "There would be a roof above our heads. The man up at the lake had to break a lock. We can do the same."

I swung the car around in the middle of the block. There was no one coming either way and there was no danger.

"You remember where it is?" she asked.

"I think I do," I said.

I missed it by a block or two and doubled back and there it was—no sign, no light of any kind, not anyone around.

"Bought and closed up," I said. "Closed up quick and easy. Not like an apartment house, where notice must be given."

"You think so?" asked Joy. "You think Atwood bought this place?"

"Why else would it be closed?" I demanded. "If it were owned by someone else, don't you think it would be open? With business as it is."

I turned into the driveway and went down a little incline. The headlights swept across another car, parked before a unit.

"Someone ahead of us," said Joy.

"Don't worry," I told her. "It's perfectly all right."

I drove across the courtyard and stopped the car with its lights full on the second car. Through the rain-blurred glass I saw the smudge of white and startled faces, looking out at us.

I sat there for a moment, then stepped out of the car. The driver's door of the other car came open and a man got out. He walked toward me in the fan of head-lamp light.

"You looking for a place to stay?" he asked. "There isn't any place."

He was middle-aged and he was well dressed although a little rumpled. His topcoat was new and his hat was an expensive piece of headgear, and beneath the topcoat he wore a business suit. His shoes were newly shined and the fine raindrops clung to them, shining in the light.

"I know there isn't any place," he said. "I've looked. Not just tonight, but every other night."

I shook my head at him and my stomach tried to roll into a hard and shrunken ball. I was sick at the sight of him. Here was another one.

"Sir," he said, "can you tell me what is going on? You're not a police officer, are you? I don't care if you are."

"I'm not a cop," I told him.

His words were edged with something that was close to hysteria—the voice of a man who had taken about everything he could. A man who had seen his own personal world fall to pieces, bit by bit, a little more each day, and absolutely helpless to do anything about it.

"I'm just a man like you," I said. "Looking for a stable."

For I'd suddenly recalled what Joy had said about no room in the inn.

It was a screwy thing to say, but he didn't seem to notice.

"My name," he said, "is John A. Quinn and I'm a vice-president of an insurance company. My salary is close to forty thousand, and here I stand without a place to live, without a place for my family to get out of the rain. Except in the car, that is."

He looked at me. "That's a laugh," he said. "Go ahead and laugh."

"I wouldn't laugh," I said. "You couldn't make me laugh."

"We sold our house almost a year ago," Quinn said "Long-term occupancy. Got a better price for it than I had any hope of getting. We needed a bigger place, you see. The family was growing up. Hated to sell our place. Nice place. Used to it. But we needed room."

I nodded. It was the same old story.

"Look," I said, "let's not stand out here in the rain."

But it was as if he hadn't heard me. He felt the need to talk. He was full of talk that needed to get out Maybe I was the first man he could really talk to, another man like himself, hunting for a shelter.

"We never thought about it," he said. "We thought it would be simple. With long-term occupancy, we had a lot of time to go out and find the kind of place we wanted. But we never found one. There were ads, of course. But we always were too late. The places had been sold before we even got there. So we tried a builder, and there wasn't any builder who could promise us a house quicker than two years. I even tried a bribe or two and it did no good. All booked up, they said. There were a lot of them who had a hundred or more houses waiting to be built. That seems incredible, doesn't it?"

"It surely does," I said.

"They said if they could get more workmen, they could build for me. But there weren't any workmen. All of them were busy. All of them had jobs.

"We put off the occupancy date, first thirty days, then sixty, and finally ninety, but there came the day we had to give possession. I offered the purchaser five thousand if he'd cancel the sale, but he wouldn't do it. Said that he was sorry but that he'd bought the house and that he needed it. Said he'd given me three months longer than had been agreed. And he was right, of course.

"We had nowhere to go. No relatives we could ask to take us in. None here, at least. We could have sent the kids to some relatives out of town, but we hated to break up the family, and some of the relatives were having troubles of their own. Lots of friends, of course, but you can't ask your friends to let you share their house. You can't even let them know what sort of shape you're in. There's such a thing as pride. You keep up the best face that you can and hope it will blow over.

"I tried everything, of course. The hotels and motels were filled up. There were no apartments. I tried to buy a trailer. There was a waiting list. God Almighty, a five-year waiting list."

"So you are here tonight," I said.

"Yes," he told me. "At least it's off the street and quiet. No passing cars to wake you up. No people walking by. It's tough. Tough on the wife and kids. We've been living in this car for almost a month. We eat in restaurants when we can, but they usually are full up. Mostly we eat at drive-ins or sometimes we buy some stuff and go out into the country and have a picnic. Picnics once were fun, but they aren't now. Even the kids don't seem to care for them. We use service stations for sanitary purposes. We do our wash at launderettes. I drive to work each morning; then the wife drives the kids to school. Then she hunts for a place to live until it's time to pick up the kids again. Then they all come to the office and pick me up and we look for a place to eat.

"We've stood it for a month," he said. "We can't take it too much longer. The kids are asking when we'll have a house again and winter's coming on. We can't live in a car when the weather turns cold, when it starts to snow. If we can't find someplace to live, we'll have to move to some other city where we can find a house, an apartment, almost anything. I'll have to give up my job and—"

"It won't do you any good," I told him. "There is no place to go. It's the same all over. It's like this everywhere."

"Mister," said Quinn, desperation pushing his voice to a higher pitch, "tell me what is wrong. What is going on?"

"I'm not sure," I said, for I couldn't tell him. It would have only made it worse. Tonight he would be better not to know.

And this, I thought, is the way it is going to be, all over. The world's population would become nomadic, wandering here and there to try to find that better place when there was no better place. First in family groups, and later, maybe, banding into tribes. Eventually a lot of them would be herded into reservations, or what would amount to reservations, as the only way that existing governments could take care of them. But until the end there would be wanderers, fighting for a roof, scrounging for a scrap of food. To start with, in the first mad rush of anger, they might seize any kind of shelter—their own houses or someone else's house. At first they would fight for food, would steal it and would hoard it. But the aliens would burn the houses or otherwise destroy them. They would destroy them as their rightful owners and there would be little that could be done about it since it would not be done openly. But the aliens would salve their social conscience because they'd consider it to be legal and the burning would go on. And there was no way to fight back against them, or at least no way that could be found immediately. For you could not fight the Atwoods, you could not battle bowling balls. You could only hate them. They would be hard to catch and they would be hard to kill and they'd have nearby ratholes into another world to which they could retreat.

There would come a time when there were no houses and when there was no food, although Man, perhaps, would linger on in spite of everything. But where there'd been a thousand men there'd now be only one, and when that day arrived the aliens would have won a war that never had been fought. Man would become a skulker on the planet he had owned.

"Mister," said the man, "I don't know your name."

"My name is Graves," I said.

"All right, Graves, what is the answer? What are we to do?"

"What you should have done from the very first," I said. "We're going to break in. You and your family will sleep beneath a roof, have a place to cook, have a bathroom of your own."

"But breaking in!" he said.

And there it was, I thought. Even in the face of desperation, a man still held regard for the laws of property. You do not steal, you don't break in, you don't touch a thing that belongs to someone else. And it was this very thing which had brought us where we were. It was these very laws, so revered that we still obeyed them even when they had turned into a trap that would take our birthright from us.

"You need a place for your kids to sleep," I said. "You need a place to shave."

"But someone will be around and—"

"If someone comes around," I said, "and tries to push you out, use a gun on them."

"I haven't got a gun," he said.

"Get one, then," I told him. "First thing in the morning."

And I was surprised at how smoothly and how easily I had slipped from a law abiding citizen into another man, quite ready to write another law and stand or fall by it.

29

The sun was slanting down between the slats on the Venetian blinds, shining into the silence and the warmth and comfort of a room I could not immediately recall.

I lay there with my eyes half open, not thinking, not wondering, not doing anything, just glad to be lying there. There was the sunlight and the silence and the softness of the bed and faint hint of perfume.

And that perfume, I thought to myself, was the kind that Joy wore.

"Joy!" I said suddenly, sitting up in bed, for now it all came back—the night and the rain and everything that had happened.

The door to the adjoining room stood open, but there was no sign of anyone.

"Joy!" I cried, tumbling out of bed.

The floor was cold when I put my feet on it, and there was a bit of chilliness in the breeze that blew through the barely open window.

I went to the door of the adjoining room and looked in. The bed had been slept in and had not been made, except that someone had pulled up the blanket. There was no sign of Joy. And then I saw the note on the door, stuck there with a pin.

I jerked it off and read:

Dear Parker: I took the car and went to the office. A story for the Sunday paper that I have to check. I'll be back this afternoon. And where is that vaunted manhood? You never even made a pass at me. Joy.

I went back and sat down on the edge of the bed, still holding the note. My trousers and shirt and jacket were draped across a chair and my shoes, with the socks stuffed inside of them, sat underneath it. Over in one corner was the rifle that I had picked up from Stirling's lab. It had been, I remembered, in the car. Joy must have gotten it out of there and brought it in and left it before she set out for the office.

I'll be back this afternoon, she'd written. And her bed was still unmade. As if she had accepted that this was the way we'd live from now on. As if there were, in fact, no other way of life. As if she already had adjusted to the changes that had come.

And Man, himself, perhaps would adjust as easily as at first, happy to find any solution out of the bitter harassment and the shattering of his hope. But after that first temporary adjustment would come the anger and the bitterness and the realization of his loss and hopelessness.

Joy had gone back to the office to check on a Sunday story. The man next door had kept on working at his insurance job even at a time when his personal world had been falling apart about him. And, of course, one had to do these things, for one had to eat, one had to live somehow, one had to have the money. But it was, I thought, perhaps a great deal more than that. It was one way, perhaps the only way that was left, to hang on to reality, to tell one's self that only a part of life had changed, that some of the old and ordered routine of one's life had not been disturbed.

And I, I asked myself—what was I to do?

I could go back to the office and sit down at my desk and try to turn out a few more columns against my coming trip. It was funny when I thought about the trip, for I'd forgotten all about it. It was almost as if it were something new, something I'd never known about before, or, if I had known of it, something from so long ago that it was natural I should have forgotten it.

I could go back to the office, but what would be the purpose? To write columns that would be never read in a paper that in a few more days might be no longer printed?

It all was so damned futile. It was something you didn't want to think about. And maybe that was why no one would listen, for if people didn't know about it, they need not think of it.

I dropped Joy's note and it fluttered to the floor. I reached out to the chair and got my shirt. And even then I didn't know what I was going to do, but before I did anything I had to get my clothes on.

I went outside and stood on the stoop and it was a fine, sunshiny day, more like a summer than an autumn day. The rain had disappeared and the court was dry again, with only a tiny puddle here and there to show it had ever rained.

I looked at my watch and it was almost noon.

The insurance man's car stood before the second unit down, but there was no sign of him or his family. It was Saturday and probably his day off and the family must be sleeping late. They had it coming to them, I told myself—a little decent rest with a roof above their heads.

Up the street I saw a restaurant sign and realized that I was hungry. And there probably was a phone there and I should call Joy.

It was just a little quick and greasy, but the place was crowded. I wriggled my way through and grabbed a stool up against the counter when a man finished and moved out.

The waitress came and I gave my order, then got up and made my way through the crowd again to the phone booth in one corner. I managed to squeeze in and get the door closed behind me. I fed in my coin and dialed. When the operator answered, I asked for Joy.

"Get that story checked?" I asked her.

"Sleepyhead," she chided. "When did you get up?"

"Just a while ago. What is going on?"

"Gavin's in a tizzy. There's a story and he can't get his mitts on it."

"Something about—"

"I don't know," said Joy, apparently knowing what I was about to ask. "Maybe. There's a money shortage in the banks. We know—"

"A money shortage! Dow told me yesterday they were knee-deep in money."

"I guess that was true," she said. "But not any more. A lot of it is gone. They had it at noon yesterday, but when they closed up last night great chunks of it had simply disappeared."

"No one will talk," I guessed.

"That's exactly it. The ones Gavin and Dow can get hold of stay absolutely mum. They don't know a thing. A lot of them—the big, important ones—they can't reach at all. You know how bankers are on Saturday. You can't get hold of them."

"Yeah," I said. "Out playing golf or fishing."

"Parker, do you think Atwood could somehow be involved?"

"I don't know," I said. "I wouldn't be surprised. I'll do some checking."

"What can you do?" she asked a little sharply.

"I could go out to the Belmont place. Atwood said—"

"I don't like it," she told me bluntly. "You were out there once before."

"I'll keep out of trouble. I can handle Atwood."

"You haven't got a car."

"I can take a cab."

"You haven't money for a cab."

"The cabby'll take me out," I said. "And he'll bring me back. On the way back, he can stop at the office and I'll pick up his fare."

"You think of everything," she said.

"Well, almost everything."

I wondered, as I hung up, if I thought of anything.

30

The first thing that I noticed was that the window had been closed. When I had fled the place the night before I had left it open, but not without the ridiculous feeling that, despite everything, I should go back and shut it.

But the window now was closed and there were draperies at the windows and I tried to recall, but with no success, whether there had been draperies there before.

The house stood old and gaunt in the pale sunlight, and from the east I could hear the distant sound of water lapping on the shore. I stood and looked at the house and there was nothing, I kept telling myself, for me to be afraid of. It was just an old and ordinary house, its gaunt bones softened by the sunlight.

"You want," the driver asked, "that I should wait for you?"

"I won't be long," I told him.

"Look, Mac, it's up to you. I don't care. The meter keeps on running."

I went up the walk. Underneath my feet, the dried and fallen leaves crunched on the paving brick.

First I'd try the door, I decided. I'd do it civilized and decent. And if no one answered when I rang the bell, then I'd go through the window as I had before. The cabdriver, more than likely, would wonder what I might be up to. But it was none of his damn business. All he had to do was wait and take me back.

Although, I told myself, someone had closed the window and now it might be locked. But that wouldn't stop me. There was nothing that was going to stop me now. Although, I realized, if I'd taken time enough to figure out why I wanted to get in, what possible reason I had for wanting to see Atwood, I'd probably find no answers. Instinct? I wondered. Joy had said something about the human instinct—or had it been Atwood who'd said it? I could not remember. Was it, then, instinct that drove me up the walk to see Atwood once again—not knowing why, not with the least idea of what I'd say to him or what purpose I might have in the saying of it?

I mounted the step and rang the bell and waited. And as I put out my finger to ring it once again, I heard footsteps in the hall.

And the bell, I remembered, had been out of order when I'd been here the night before. It had been loose and had wobbled underneath my finger when I had tried to ring it. But now it was all right and the window had been closed and there were footsteps in the hall, coming toward the door.

The door came open and a girl stood there, dressed in the stark black-and-whiteness of a maid's uniform.

I just stood and stared.

The maid stood without moving, waiting for me. There was a pert look on her face.

"I had hoped," I finally said, "to find Mr. Atwood here."

"Sir," she said, "won't you please come in?"

I stepped into the hall and there was a difference there as well. Last night the house had been dusty and untenanted, with covers over what little furniture there was. But now the place had a lived-in look. The dust was gone and the wood and tile of the hall shone with cleanliness and polish. There was an ancient hall tree, standing lone and empty, and beside it was a full-length mirror that gleamed with recent washing.

"Your hat and coat, sir," said the maid. "Madam's in the study."

"But Atwood. It was Atwood—"

"Mr. Atwood is not here, sir."

She took my hat out of my hand. She waited for the coat.

I took it off and handed it to her.

"That way, sir," she said.

The door was open and I walked through it, into a room where books jammed shelves from floor to ceiling. At the desk beside the windows sat the icy blonde I'd met in the bar, the one who'd handed me the card that said "We Deal in Everything."

"Good day, Mr. Graves," she said. "I am glad you came."

"Atwood told me—"

"Mr. Atwood, unfortunately, is not with us any more."

"And you, of course, are about to take his place."

The iciness was there, and the smell of violets. She was part blond goddess, part efficient secretary. And she was, as well, a thing from another world and a tiny, perfect doll I'd held within my hands.

"You are astounded, Mr. Graves?"

"No," I said. "Not now. Once perhaps. But not any longer."

"You came to talk with Mr. Atwood. We had hoped that you would come. We have need of people like you."

"You need me," I said, "like I need an extra head."

"Mr. Graves, won't you have a chair? And please don't be facetious."

I sat down in the chair just across the desk from her.

"What do you want me to do?" I asked. "Should I break down and weep?"

"There is no need of your doing anything," she said. "Please just be yourself. Let us talk exactly as if we were two humans."

"Which, of course, you're not."

"No, Mr. Graves, I'm not."

We sat there looking at one another and it was damned uncomfortable. There wasn't a flicker of movement or emotion in her face: it was just graven beauty.

"If you were a different kind of man," she said, "I'd try to make you forget I am anything but human. But I don't suppose it would do me any good with you."

I shook my head. "I'm sorry about it, too," I told her. "Believe me, I am sorry. I would like nothing better than to think of you as human."

"Mr. Graves, if I were human, that would be the nicest compliment I ever had been paid."

"And since you're not?"

"I believe it's still a compliment."

I looked sharply at her. It was not only what she'd said hut the way she'd said it. "Maybe, after all," I said, "there may be some human in you."

"No," she said. "Let's not start kidding ourselves, either one of us. Basically you should hate me, and I suppose you do. Although maybe not entirely. And basically I should have a great contempt for you, but I can't say honestly I do. And yet, I think, we should talk together, if possible, with some rationality."

"Why be rational with me? There are a lot of others—"

"But, Mr. Graves," she said, "you know about us. And few of the others do. A very, very few throughout the entire world. You'd be surprised how few."

"And I'm to keep my mouth shut."

"Really, Mr. Graves. You know better than all that. How many people have you found so far who would listen to you?"

"Exactly one," I told her.

"That would be the girl. You're in love with her and she's in love with you."

I nodded.

"So, you see," she said, "the only acceptance for your story has been emotional."

"I suppose that you could say so." I felt like an utter fool.

"So let's be businesslike," she said. "Let us say we're giving you a chance to make the best bargain that you can. We'd not have approached you if you'd not known of us, but since you do, there's nothing to be lost."

"Bargain?" I asked stupidly.

"Why, of course," she told me. "You're in on—what do you call it? The ground floor; is that right?"

"But, perhaps, on a deal like this—"

"Listen, Mr. Graves. You must not have illusions. I suspect you do, but you must get rid of them. There is no way you can stop us. There's nothing that can stop us. The operation has simply gone too far. There was a time, perhaps, when you could have stopped us. But not any longer. Believe me, Mr. Graves, it is far too late."

"Since it is too late, why do you bother with me?"

"We have use of you," she said. "There are certain things that you can do for us. The humans, once they know what is going on, are going to resent what is being done to them. Is that not right, Mr. Graves?"

"Sister," I told her, "you don't know the half of it."

"But we, you understand, want to have no trouble. Or as little trouble as is possible. We feel that we stand on firm moral and legal ground, that we have abided by all the injunctions set up by your own society. We have violated none of the rules and we have no wish to be forced to go through a program of pacification. I am sure the humans would not want it, either, for it can become, I must assure you, very, very painful. We want to get this project finished and go on to something else. We want to terminate it as smoothly as lies within our power. And you can help us do that."

"But why should I?"

"Mr. Graves," she said, "you would be performing a service, not for us alone, but for the human race as well. Anything that you can do to make this go smoothly for us would be of benefit to your people, too. For no matter what they do, their fate in the end will be the very same. There is no reason for them to be subjected to unnecessarily harrowing experiences to achieve that end. Consider this: you are an expert in mass communications—"

"Not as expert as you think," I said.

"But you know the methods and the techniques. You can write convincingly . . ."

"There are others who would be more convincing."

"But, Mr. Graves, you are the one we have."

I didn't like the way she said it.

"What you want me to do," I said, "is keep the people quiet. Keep them lulled asleep."

"That, and any counsel you may have about how we should react in different situations. A consultative position, you might say."

"But you know. You know as well as I do."

"You are thinking, Mr. Graves, perhaps, that we have absorbed the human viewpoint in its entirety. That we can think as humans think and act as humans act. But this is simply not the case. We know what you call business, certainly. Perhaps you would agree that we know it rather thoroughly. We are well versed in your laws. But there are many areas we have not had the time to study. We know human nature only to a point—insofar as it reacts in the world of commerce. But we know it otherwise most imperfectly. We have no good idea how the humans will react when they learn the truth."

"Cold feet?" I asked.

"No, we haven't got cold feet. We are prepared to be as ruthless as may be necessary. But it would take time. We don't want to take the time."

"OK. So I write the stuff for you. What good would it do to write it? Who would publish it? How would you get it to the people?"

"Write it," said this blond iceberg. "We'll take it on from there. We'll get it to the people. We'll distribute it. That is not your worry."

I was afraid. Perhaps a little angry. But mostly afraid. For not until this moment had I really realized the sheer implacability of these aliens. They were not vindictive and they were not hateful. They were scarcely an enemy in the sense we used the word. They were a malignant force and there was no pleading that would move them. They simply did not care. To them the Earth was no more than a piece of property and the humans less than nothing.

"You're asking me," I said, "to be a traitor to my race."

Even as I said it, I was well aware that the term of traitor was meaningless to them. Recognized in its proper context, more than likely, but without a shred of meaning. For these things would not have the same kind of ethics as the human race; they would have another set of ethics, probably, but a set that would be as far beyond our comprehension as ours had been to them.

"Let's think of it," she said, "in practical terms. We're giving you a choice. You either go along with the rest of humanity and share their common fate or you go along with us and fare a good deal better. If you decline, you will not hurt us greatly. If you accept, you'll help yourself, to a great extent, and your fellow humans, perhaps to a somewhat less extent. You stand to gain and, believe me, the human race can't lose."

"How do I know you'll keep your bargain?"

"A bargain is a bargain," she said stiffly.

"You'll pay well, I suppose."

"Very well," she said.

One of the bowling balls, coming out of nowhere I could see, rolled across the floor. It stopped about three feet from where I was sitting in the chair.

The girl got up from behind the desk and came around it She stood at one corner of it, looking at the bowling ball.

The ball became striated—finely striated, like a diffraction grating. Then it began to split along all those tiny lines. It turned from black to green and split, and instead of a bowling ball, there was a little heap of money piled upon the floor.

I didn't say a word. I couldn't say a word.

She stooped and picked up a bill and handed it to me. I looked at it. She waited. I looked at it some more. "Well, Mr. Graves?" she said.

"It looks like money," I told her.

"It is money. How else do you think we got all the money that we needed?"

"And you did it by the rules," I said.

"I don't know what you mean."

"You broke one rule. The most important rule of all. Money is a measure of what one has done—of the road he had built or the picture he had painted or the hours he has worked."

"It's money," she said. "That is all that's needed."

She bent again and scooped up the entire pile of it. She put it on the desk and began to stack it

There was no point, I knew, in trying to make her understand. She wasn't being cynical. Or dishonest. It was a lack of understand-ing—an alien blind spot Money was a product, not a symbol. It could be nothing else.

She made neat piles of it. She stooped and picked up the few stray bills that had fluttered off the pile when she had picked it up. She put the stray bills on the pile.

The bill I had in my hand was a twenty, and a lot of the others seemed to be twenties, too, although there were some tens and a stray fifty here and there.

She stacked all the piles together and held it out to me.

"It's yours," she said.

"But I haven't said—"

"Whether you work for us or not, it's yours. And you'll think about what I've been telling you."

"I'll think about it," I said.

I stood up and took the money from her. I stuffed it in my pock-ets. The pockets bulged with it.

"There will come a day," I said, patting the pockets, "when this stuff is no longer any good. There'll be a time when there'll be noth-ing one can buy with it."

"When that day comes," she said, "there will be something else. There'll be whatever you may need."

I stood there thinking, and the only thing that I could think about was that now I had the money to pay the taxi driver. Except for that, my mind was a total blank. The enormity of this meeting had wiped me clean of everything except a total sense of loss—that and the fact that now I could pay the driver.

I had to get out of there, I knew. Had to leave this place before the flood of revulsion and emotion should come crashing down upon me. I had to leave while I still could leave with a numbed human dignity. I had to get away and find a place and the time to think. And until I did this thinking, I must appear to go along with them.

"I thank you, miss," I said. "I don't seem to know your name."

"I haven't got a name," she told me. "There was never any reason I should have a name. Only ones like Atwood had to have a name."

"I thank you, then," I said. "I will think it over."

She turned and walked out of the room into the entry hall. There was no sign of the maid. Beyond the hall I saw that the living room was clean and shining and filled with furniture. And how much of it, I wondered, was really furniture, and how much of it was bowling balls changed into furniture?

I picked my coat and hat off the hall tree.

She opened the front door.

"It was nice of you to come," she said. "It was very thoughtful. I trust you'll come again."

I walked out of the door and did not see my cab. In its place stood a long, white Cadillac.

"I had a cab," I said. "It must be down the road."

"We paid off the driver," said the girl, "and sent him on his way. You will not need a cab."

She saw my befuddlement.

"The car is yours," she said. "If you're to work with us—"

"With a built-in bomb?" I asked.

She sighed. "How do I make you understand? Let me put it brutally. So long as you can be useful to us, no harm will come to you. Perform this service for us and harm will never come to you. You'll be taken care of as long as you may live."

"And Joy Kane?" I asked.

"If you wish. Joy Kane as well."

She looked at me with her icy eyes. "But try to stop us now, try to cross us now . . ."

She made a sound like a knife going through a throat.

I went down to the car.

31

At the edge of the city I stopped at a neighborhood shopping center and walked to a drugstore to buy a paper. I wanted to see if Gavin had been able to get his story about the missing bank funds.

I could tell him now, I knew, exactly what had happened. But, just like the others, he wouldn't listen to me. I could walk into the office and sit down at my desk and write the greatest story the world had ever known. But it would be a waste of time to do it. It would not be published. It would be too ridiculous to publish. And even if it were published, no one would believe it. Or almost no one. A crackpot here and there. Not enough to count.

Before I got out of the car I riffled through the money in my jacket pocket to find a ten-dollar bill. I looked for a five and there weren't any. And there weren't any ones.

I wondered, as I riffled through it, how much money I might have. Not that it mattered greatly. Just curiosity.

For money in a few more weeks, perhaps in a few more days, would begin to lose its value. And a short time after that the value would be lost. It would be no more than so much worthless paper. You couldn't eat it and you couldn't wear it and it would not shelter you from the wind or weather. For it was no more—had never been more—than a tool devised by Man to carry out his peculiar system of culture and of life. It had no more significance, actually, than the notches on the gun butt or the crude marks chalked upon the wall. It had been no more, at any time, than sophisticated counters.

I walked into the drugstore and picked a paper off the pile on top of the cigar counter and there, staring out at me, all grins and full of happiness, was a picture of the Dog.

There could be no doubt about it. I'd have known him anywhere. He sat there, bubbling with good-fellowship, and behind him was the White House.

The headline beneath the picture was the clincher. It said:

TALKING DOG ARRIVES TO VISIT PRESIDENT

"Mister," said the clerk, "do you want that paper?"
I gave him the bill and he groused about it.
"That the smallest that you got?"
I told him that it was.

He gave me the change and I stuffed it and the paper in my pocket and went back to the car. I wanted to read the story, but for some reason I did not understand, or even try to understand, I wanted to get back to the car to do it, to where I could sit and read it without the possibility of someone disturbing me.

The story was cute, just a shade too cute.

It told about this dog that had come to see the President, He'd trotted through the gate before anyone could stop him and he'd tried to get into the White House, but the guards had shoved him out. He went reluctantly, trying to explain, in his doggish manner, that he wanted to make no trouble but would be very much obliged if he could see the President. He tried to get in a couple of more times, and finally the guards put in a call to the dogcatcher.

The catcher came and got the dog, who went along with him willingly enough, without apparent malice. And in a little while the catcher came back and the dog was with him. The catcher explained to the guards that maybe it would be a good idea if they did let the dog see the President. The dog, he said, had talked to him, explaining that it was most important he see the chief executive.

So the guards went to the phone again and in a little while someone came and got the dogcatcher and took him to a hospital, where he still was under observation. The dog was allowed to stay, however, and one of the guards explained to him most emphatically that it was ridiculous of him to expect to see the President.

He was, the story said, polite and well behaved. He sat outside the White House and didn't bother anything. He didn't even chase the squirrels on the White House lawn.

"This reporter," said the story, "tried to talk with him. We asked him several questions, but he never said a word. He just grinned at us."

And there he was, in the picture on page one, just as big as life— a shaggy, friendly bum that no one for a moment would think of taking seriously.

But, perhaps, I thought, you couldn't blame the newsman who had written that story or any of the rest of them, for there was nothing quite so outrageous as a shaggy dog that talked. And, perhaps, when you came to think of it, it was no whit more ridiculous than a bunch of bowling balls about to grab the Earth.

If the threat had been bloody or spectacular, then it could be comprehended. But, as it stood, it was neither, and all the more deadly because of that very fact.

Stirling had talked about a nonenvironmental being, and that was what these aliens were. They could adapt to anything; they could assume any sort of shape; they could assimilate and use to their own advantage any kind of thinking; they could twist to their own purposes any economic, political, or social system. They were things that were completely flexible; they could adapt to any condition which might be brought about to fight them.

And it could be, I told myself, that we were not facing here many bowling balls but one giant organism that could divide and split itself into many forms for many purposes, while still remaining its single self, aware of all the things its many parts were doing.

How do you thwart a thing like that? I asked myself. How do you stand against it?

Although, even if it should be one great organism, there were certain facets to it which were hard of explanation. Why had the girl without a name, instead of Atwood, been waiting for me at the Belmont house?

We knew nothing of them and there was no time to know anything of them, or it, whichever it might be. And such a knowledge was something one must have, for surely the life and culture of this enemy must be as complex and as peculiar in its many ways as the human culture.

They could become anything at all. They could see, apparently, in some restricted sense, into future happenings. And they were in ambush and would stay in ambush as long as they were able. Was it possible, I wondered, that mankind could go crashing to its death without ever knowing what had caused its death?

And I, myself, I wondered—what was I to do?

It would have been no more than human to have thrown the money in their faces, to have hurled defiance at them. It would, perhaps, have been an easy thing to do. Although, I remembered, at the time I had been so numb with fear that I'd been able to do nothing of the sort.

And, I realized with a start, I thought of them as them, not as him or her, not as Atwood, not as the girl who had no name because she'd never needed one. And did that mean, I wondered, that their human guise was thinner than it seemed?

I folded the paper and laid it on the seat beside me and slid beneath the wheel.

This was not the time for grand heroics. It was a time a man did what he could, no matter how it seemed. If, by pretending to go along with them, I could gain some fact, some insight, some hint that would help the humans, then, perhaps, that was the thing to do. And if it ever came to a point where I had to write the alien propaganda, might it not escape them if I wrote into it something that they had not intended and might not recognize but that would be crystal-clear to the human readers?

I started the engine and put the car in gear and the car slid out into the stream of traffic. It was a good car. It was the finest thing I had ever driven. In spite of where it came from, in spite of everything, I felt proud of driving it.

Back at the motel, Quinn's car still was parked in front of his unit, and now there were two other cars parked in front of other units. Soon, I knew, the motel would be full. People would drive in and say to other people there how do you go about getting lodging here. And the people there would say you use a crowbar or sledgehammer and they might even, then, produce a bar or hammer and help them to break in. For the moment, at least, people would stick together. In adversity, they'd help one another. It only would be later that they would fall apart, each one on his own. And later, after that perhaps, come back together, knowing once again that human strength lay in unity.

When I got out of the car, Quinn came out of his unit and walked over to meet me.

"That's quite a car you have," he said.

"Belongs to a friend of mine," I told him. "Get a good night's sleep?"

He grinned. "Best in weeks. And the wife is happy. It isn't very much, of course, but it's the best we've had in a good long time."

"See we have some neighbors."

He nodded. "They came in and asked. I told them. I went out and got a gun, the way you told me. Felt a little foolish, but it won't hurt to have it. Wanted a rifle, but all I could get was a shotgun. Just as well, I imagine. I'm no dead eye with a rifle."

"All you could get?" I asked.

"Went to three hardware stores. All of them were out. Went to a fourth and they had this shotgun. So I bought it."

So the guns, I thought, were being bought. Soon, perhaps, there'd not be any to be had. Other frightened people who felt a little safer if they could reach out their hand and pick up a weapon.

He looked down at the ground and scrubbed a pattern with the toe of his shoe.

"Funny thing happened," he said. "I haven't told the wife about it because it might upset her. Drove out to get some groceries and went out of my way to go past our house—the one we sold, I mean. First time I had driven past it since we left it. Neither had my wife. She told me several times she wanted to but didn't, because it would make her feel too bad. But, anyhow, I drove past it today. And there it was—empty, like we moved out of it. Even in this short a time beginning to look shabby. They made us get out of it a month ago and they haven't moved in yet. They said they needed it. They said they had to have it. But they didn't need it. What do you make of it?"

"I don't know," I said.

I could have told him. Maybe I should have told him. I know I wanted to. For he might have believed what I had to tell him. He had taken weeks of punishment, he was softened up, he was ready to believe. And, God knows, I needed someone to believe me—someone who could huddle with me in a little pit of fear and misery.

But I didn't tell him, for it would have served no purpose. At the moment, at least, he was far happier not knowing. Now he still had hope, for he could ascribe all that had happened to an economic malady. A malady that he could not understand of course, but a misadjustment that lay within a familiar framework and one that Man could cope with.

But this other—the true—explanation of it would have left him without hope and facing the unknowable. And that would spell pure panic.

If I could have made a million people understand, then it would have been all right, for out of that million there would have been a few who would have viewed it calmly and objectively and given leadership. But to tell it to a little puddle of people in a single city had no point at all.

"It makes no sense," said Quinn. "The whole thing makes no sense. I've laid awake at night to get it figured out and there's no way to figure it. But that's not the reason I came out. We would like to have you and the wife eat dinner with us. It won't be too much, but we have a roast and I could fix a drink or two. We could sit and talk."

"Mr. Quinn," I said, "Joy is not my wife. We are just two people who got sort of thrown together."

"Well," he said, "I'm sorry. I had just presumed she was. It really makes no difference. I hope you're not embarrassed."

"Not at all," I said.

"And you will eat with us?"

"Some other time," I said. "But thank you very much. I may have a lot to do."

He stood there and looked at me. "Graves," he said, "there's something that you haven't told me. Something about this business you said the other night. You said it was the same all over, that there was no place to run. How did you know that?"

"I'm a newspaperman," I told him. "I'm working on a story."

"And you do know something."

"Not very much," I said.

He waited and I didn't tell him. He flushed and turned around. "Be seeing you," he said, and went back to his unit.

I didn't blame him any. I felt like a heel myself.

I went into the unit and there was no one there. Joy was still at the office. Gavin, more than likely, had found things for her to do.

I took the greater part of the money out of my pockets and hid it underneath the mattress on my bed. Not too imaginative or too good a place, but no one knew I had it and I wasn't worried. I had to put it somewhere. I couldn't leave it lying out where anyone could see it.

I picked up the rifle and took it out and put it in the car.

Then I did something I'd been intending to do ever since I'd left the Belmont place.

I went over the car. I went over all of it. I lifted the hood and checked the motor. I crawled beneath it and checked it entirely out. There wasn't a part of it I failed to examine.

And when I had finished, there could be no doubt.

It was what it was supposed to be. It was an expensive but entirely ordinary car. There was nothing different. There wasn't a thing left out or a thing put on. There was no bomb, no malfunctioning that I could find. It wasn't, I could swear, something fashioned by the artistry of a bunch of bowling balls that had clubbed together to simulate a car. It was honest steel and glass and chrome.

I stood beside it and patted the fender and wondered what I should do next.

And maybe the thing to do, I thought, was to put in another call for Senator Roger Hill. When you get sobered up, he'd said, call me back again. If you still have something to tell me, call me back tomorrow.

And I was sober and I still had something to tell him.

I was pretty sure what he would say, but still I had to call him.

I headed for the little restaurant to call the senator.

32

Parker," said the senator, "I am glad you called."

"Maybe," I said, "you will listen to me now."

"Certainly," said the senator in that oily way of his, "if you don't insist on that cock and bull about invading aliens."

"But, Senator . . ."

"I don't mind telling you," said the senator, "that there'll be hell to pay—look, you know, of course, I'm talking off the record."

"I guessed that," I told him. "When you come up with something interesting, it's always off the record."

"Well, there'll be hell to pay come Monday morning when the market opens. We don't know what's happened, but the banks are short of money. Not one bank, mind you, but damn near every bank. There's not a one of them that can get its cash to balance. Every bank right now has its people in on overtime to find out where all that cash went to. But that is not the worst of it."

"What is the worst of it?"

"That money," said the senator. "There was too much of it to start with. A way too much of it. You take the cash on hand as of Friday morning and add it up and there is more of it, a good deal more of it, than there had any right to be. There isn't that much money, I tell you, Parker, in the whole United States."

"But it's not there any more."

"No," said the senator, "it's not there anymore. The money, so far as we can figure out, is back to somewhere near the figure one would expect to see."

I waited for him to go on, and in the little silence I heard him take a deep breath, as if he were strangling for air.

"Something else," he said. "There are rumors. Just all sorts of rumors. A new one every hour. And you can't check them out."

"What kind of rumors?"

He hesitated; then he said: "Remember, off the record."

"Sure, it's off the record."

"There's one rumor that someone, no one knows quite who, has grabbed control of U. S. Steel and a slew of other corporations."

"Same people?"

"God, Parker, I don't know. I don't know if there's anything to any of it or not. You hear one rumor one minute and there's another one the next."

He paused a moment; then he asked: "Parker, what do you know about this?"

I could have told him what I knew, but I knew it wasn't smart to do it. He'd just get sore and chew me out and that would be the end of it.

"I can tell you what to do," I said. "What you have to do."

"I hope it's a good idea."

"Pass a law," I said.

"If we passed every law—"

"A law," I said, "outlawing private ownership. Every sort of private ownership. Make it so that no one can own a foot of ground, an industrial plant, an ounce of ore, a house—"

"Are you crazy!" yelled the senator. "You can't pass that kind of law. You can't even think about it."

"And while you're at it, dream up a substitute for money."

The senator sputtered without making any words.

"Because," I said, "the way it is, the aliens are buying up the Earth. If you leave it as it is, they will own the Earth."

The senator got his voice back.

"Parker," he yelled, "you are off your rocker. I have never heard such damn foolishness as this in all my life and I've heard a lot of it."

"If you don't believe me, go and ask the Dog."

"What the hell has a dog got to do with this? What dog?"

"The one down at the White House. Waiting to get in and see the President."

"Parker," he snapped, "don't call me again. I have enough on my mind without listening to you. I don't know what you're trying to do. But don't call me again. If this is a joke—"

"It's not a joke," I said.

"Good-bye, Parker," said the senator.

"Good-bye, Senator," I said.

I hung up the receiver and stood in the little cubicle, trying to think.

It all was utterly hopeless, I knew. The senator had been, from the start, the only hope I had. He was the only man I knew in public office who had imagination, but I guess not enough imagination to listen to what I had to tell him.

I had done my best, I thought, and it had been no good. Perhaps if I'd done it differently, if I'd gone about it differently, it might have worked out better. But a man could say that about anything he did. And there was no way of knowing. It was done now and there was no way of knowing.

There was nothing now that could stop what the aliens had begun. And it apparently was coming sooner than I thought. Monday morning would bring a panic in Wall Street and the economy would start to fall apart. The first crack in our financial structure would begin on the trading floor and would go fast from there. In the space of one week's time, the world would be in chaos.

And more than likely, I thought, with a cold chill down my spine, the aliens knew what I had done. It was inconceivable that they'd not be somehow tied in with the communications systems. They would know I'd called the senator even as I was supposed to be considering their offer.

It was something I'd not thought of. There were too many things to think of. But even if I'd thought of it, I still probably would have put in the call.

Perhaps it would make no great difference to them. Maybe they had expected that I'd flounder around a bit before I agreed to take the job they'd offered. And thus the call, by once again demonstrating to me the impossibility of what I was trying to accomplish, might, to their way of thinking, bind me closer to them, convinced finally that there was no way in which one might resist them.

Were there other things to do? Other approaches that a man might take? Was there anything a man could do at all?

I could call the President, or I could try to call him. I didn't kid myself. I knew how little chance there'd be for me to talk with him. Especially at a time like this, when the President had the greatest burden any man in office had faced since the beginning of the nation.

See the Dog, I'd tell him, when and if I got him on the line. See the Dog that's waiting out there for you.

It wouldn't work. There was no way to make it work.

I was beat, hands down. I'd never had a chance. There'd be no one who had a chance.

I found a dime and fed it into the slot.

I dialed the office and asked for Joy.

"Everything all right?" she asked.

"Everything's just fine. When are you coming home?"

"I don't know," she said angrily. "This damn Gavin, he finds more, things to do."

"Just walk out on him."

"You know I can't do that."

"Well, all right, then. Where do you want to eat tonight? Think of an expensive place. I'm loaded."

"How come you are loaded? I have your check right here. I picked it up for you."

"Joy, believe me, I have wads of cash. Where do you want to eat?"

"Let's not go out," she said. "Let us cook a meal. The restaurants are so crowded."

"Steaks? What else? I'll go out and get it."

She told me what else.

I went out to get it.

33

I came back to the car, packing one of those oversize grocery bags filled with all the stuff Joy had ticked off for me.

The car was far down the line in the supermarket parking lot and the bag was heavy and packed rather sloppily and there were a couple of cans, one of corn and another one of peaches, that had started to tear a hole in the bottom of the bag and were trying to get out.

I padded across the lot, walking carefully so as not to joggle the bag more than necessary, clutching it desperately with both hands in an earnest attempt to keep it from breaking up entirely.

I reached the car without disaster but on the very verge of it. By a process of contortionist acrobatics I got the front door open and dumped the bag onto the seat. It came apart then, spilling all the groceries into a jumbled heap. I used both hands to shove the mess to the other side so I could get underneath the wheel.

I suppose that if I'd not been having so much trouble with the bag of groceries, I'd have noticed it at once, but I didn't see it until I had gotten in and was reaching out to insert the key in the ignition lock.

And there it was, a sheet of paper, folded to make a tent and propped above the instrument panel and against the windshield.

Across the sheet had been printed in large block letters the single word "STINKER!"

I had leaned forward to put the key into the lock and I stayed leaning forward, staring at the paper and its one-word message.

I didn't even have to guess who might have put it there. There was no doubt in my mind. It was almost as if I knew, as if I'd seen them put it there—some pseudo-human, some agglomeration of the bowling balls that had made themselves into a human form, telling me they knew I had called the senator, telling me they knew I would double-cross them if I had the chance. Not angry with me, perhaps, not particularly disturbed at what I'd done, but disgusted with me, perhaps—perhaps disappointed in me. Something just to let me know they were on to me and that I was not getting away with anything.

I shoved the key into the lock and started the engine. I reached out and got the paper and crumpled it into a ball and tossed it out the window. If they were watching me, and I figured that they were, that would let them know what I thought of them.

Childish? Sure, it was. I just didn't give a damn. There was nothing left to give a damn about

Three blocks down the street, I noticed the car. It was just an ordinary car, black and medium-priced. I don't know why I noticed it. There was nothing unusual about it. It was the kind of car, the age, the make, the color you saw a hundred times a day.

Perhaps the answer is that I would have noticed any car that pulled in behind me.

I went two more blocks and it still trailed along behind. I made a couple of turns and it still was there.

There was little question that it was tailing me, and a clumsy job of tailing.

I headed out of town and it followed still, half a block behind. Not caring, I thought, not even trying to hide the fact that it was following. Wanting me to know, perhaps, that I was being followed, just keeping on the pressure.

I wondered, as I drove, whether I should even bother to shake this follower. There didn't seem to be any particular reason that I should. Even if I shook him, it might make little difference. There wasn't much, I told myself, to be gained by it. They had monitored my call to the senator. More than likely they knew my base of operations, if you could so dignify it. Without much question, they knew exactly where to find me if they ever wanted me.

But there might be some small advantage; I told myself, if I could make them think that I didn't know all this. It was a good, cheap way of playing dumb, for whatever that was worth.

I reached the city limits and hit one of the west highways and let out the car a bit. I gained on my pursuer, but not by very much.

Ahead the road curved up a hill, with a sharper curve starting at the top. Leading off the curve, I remembered, was a country road. There was little traffic, and maybe, if I were lucky, I could duck into the side road and be out of sight before the black car cleared the curve.

I gained a little on him on the hill and put on a burst of speed when he was hidden by the curve. The road ahead was clear, and as I reached the side road I slammed on the brakes and turned the wheel hard over. The car hugged the ground like a crouching animal. The rear wheels started to skid a bit, squealing on the pavement; then I was into the country road and straightened out and pouring on the gas.

The road was hilly, one steep incline and then another, with sharp dips between them. And at the top of the third of them, glancing up at the rear-vision mirror, I saw the black car topping the second hill behind.

It was a shock. Not that it meant so awfully much, but I had been so sure I had shaken him that it was a solid blow at my confidence.

It angered me as well. If that little pip-squeak back there . . .

Then I saw the trail. It was, I suppose, an old wagon road of some years ago, choked with weeds and with the branches of a grove

of trees hanging down to shield it, as if the very branches were trying to hide the faint trace that was left.

I turned the car's wheel sharply and went bumping over the shal-
low ditch. The overhanging branches blotted out the windshield
and screeched against the metal of the body.

I drove blind, with the tires bouncing in the old, almost obliter-
ated ruts. Finally I stopped and got out. The branches hung low on
the track behind, and it was unlikely that the car could be seen by
anyone passing on the road.

I grinned in minor triumph.

This time, I was sure, I had put one over.

I waited, and the black car topped the hill and came roaring
down the road. In the silence of the afternoon, it made a lot of
noise. It didn't have too far more to run before it would need a
major overhaul.

It went on down the hill; then there was a screech of brakes.
They kept on screeching for some time before the car came to a
halt.

Licked again, I thought. Somehow or other, they knew that I
was here.

So they wanted to play rough. So if that was the way they wanted
it, that was the way they'd have it.

I opened the front door and reached into the back to pick up
the rifle. I swung it in my hand, and the weight and heft of it had
an assuring feel. For a moment I wondered just how much good
the rifle might be against a thing like this; then I remembered
how Atwood had come apart when I'd reached for the pistol in
my pocket and how the car on the road up north had gone rolling
down the hillside when I'd opened fire on it.

Rifle in hand, I cat-footed down the trail. If the follower should
come hunting me—and certainly he would—it would never do to
let him find me where he thought I was.

I moved through a hushed and silent world, redolent with the
scent of autumn. Crimson-leafed vines looped above the trail, and

there was a constant rain of frost-tinted leaves, falling gently and slowly, running a slow-paced maze through the branches of the grove. Except for a slight rustling as my feet scuffed against a dry leaf here and there, walking was quiet. Years of fallen leaves and growing moss made a carpet that deadened every noise.

I came to the edge of the grove and crept along it to reach the top of the hill. I found a flaming sumac bush and squatted down behind it. The bush still held its full quota of glossy red leaves and I was in splendid ambush.

Below me the hill swept down toward a tiny stream, no more than a trickle of water that ran down the fold between the hills. The grove curved in toward the road, and below it was a brown expanse of hillside covered by high, dry weeds, with here and there the flaming fire of another sumac cluster.

The man came down the creek, then started up the long slope of hill, heading straight toward me, almost as if he knew I was hiding there behind the bush. He was an undistinguished-looking customer, a man walking with a slight stoop to his shoulders, with an old felt hat pulled down around his ears, and dressed in some sort of a black suit that even from that distance I could see was shabby.

He came straight toward me, not looking up. As if he were pretending he didn't see me, had no idea I was anywhere around. He moved at a shambling gait, and not very fast, plodding up the hill, with his eyes bent on the ground.

I brought up the gun and poked the barrel through the scarlet leaves. I held it steady on my shoulder and put the sights on the bent-down head of the man who climbed the hill.

He stopped. As if he knew the rifle had been pointed at him, he stopped and his head came up and swiveled on his neck. He straightened and he stiffened, and then he changed his course, angling across the hillside toward a little swale that was grown high with weeds.

I lowered the rifle, and as I did I caught the first edge of the tainted air.

I sniffed to be certain what I smelled, and there was no mistaking it. There was an irate skunk somewhere, down there on the hillside.

I grinned. It served him right, I thought. It served the damn fool right.

He was plunging, moving rapidly now, through the patch of waist-high weeds, down toward the swale, and then he disappeared.

I rubbed my eyes and had another look and still he wasn't there.

He might have stumbled and fallen in the weeds, I told myself, but there was the haunting feeling I'd seen it all before. I had seen it in the basement of the Belmont house. Atwood had been there, sitting in the chair, and in an instant the chair had been empty and the bowling balls had been rolling on the floor.

I had not seen it happen. I had not looked away. I could not have missed its happening and yet I had. Atwood had been there one moment and the next there'd been the bowling balls.

And this was what had happened here, in the bright sunshine of an autumn afternoon. One moment a man had been walking through the weeds and then he'd not been walking. He was nowhere to be seen.

I stood up cautiously, with the rifle held at ready, and peered down the hillside.

There was nothing to be seen except the waving weeds, and it was only in that one spot, in that spot where the man had disappeared, that the weeds were waving. All else on the entire hillside was standing deathly still.

The scent of skunk came stronger to my nostrils, drifting up the hill.

And there was something damned funny going on.

The weeds were waving wildly, as if there were something thrashing in them, but there was no sound. There was no sound at all.

I moved down the hill, with the rifle still at ready.

And suddenly there was something in my pocket, fighting to get out. As if a mouse or rat had sneaked into my pocket and now was trying to get free.

I made a wild grab at the pocket, but even as I did the thing came out of it. It was a tiny ball of black, like one of those small, soft rubber balls they give tiny kids to play with.

It popped out of my pocket and dodged my grasping fingers and fell into the grass, squirming madly through the grass, heading for that place where the weeds were waving.

I stood and watched it go and wondered what it was. And all at once I knew. It was the money. It was that part of the money I still had in my pocket—the money I had been given at the Belmont house.

Now it had changed back into what it had been before and was hurrying toward the place where that other thing, the one shaped like a man, had suddenly disappeared.

I gave a yell and rah toward the weeds, throwing aside all caution.

For there was something going on and I must find out what it was.

The scent of skunk was almost overpowering and, despite myself, I started veering off, and then I saw out of the corner of my eye what was going on.

I stopped and stared, not quite understanding.

There were bowling balls down there in the weeds, gamboling wildly and ecstatically and with complete abandon. They spun and rolled and leaped into the air.

And up out of that patch of weeds rose the nauseating eye-watering, spine-tingling smell left by a passing skunk that something had disturbed.

It was more than I could stand. I retreated, gagging.

Running for the car, I knew, in something less than triumph, that at last I'd found a chink in the bowling balls' almost perfect armor.

34

They liked perfume, the Dog had said. Once they had seized the Earth, they would barter it for a consignment of perfumes. It was the thing they lived for; it was their one and only source of pleasure. It was the thing they valued beyond all else.

And here on Earth, on a weedy swale running down an autumn hillside, they'd found one that they liked. For there was no other way in which one could interpret their ecstatic gamboling. And one, apparently, that had a strong enough appeal to force them to give up whatever purpose they might have held in mind.

I got into the car and backed it out onto the road and drove back toward the main highway.

Apparently the bowling balls, I thought, had not found the other perfumes of Earth worth particular attention, but they'd gone crazy on the skunk. And while it made no sense to me, I suppose that, naturally, it must make some sort of sense to a bowling ball.

There must be a way, I told myself, that the human race could use the newfound knowledge to advantage, some way in which we could cash in on this matter of the bowling balls' love affair with skunks.

I remembered back to the day before when Gavin had put Joy's story about the skunk farm on page one. But the skunks in that particular instance had been different kinds of skunks.

I thought around in circles, and all the thinking came to nothing. And, I thought at last, how infuriating it would be if this one sign of the alien's weakness could not serve some human purpose.

For it was, so far as I could see, the only chance we had. In every other department, they had us licked without a chance of recourse.

But if there were a way to use this thing we had, I couldn't think of one. If there had been other people, if there had been more than myself alone, I might have thought of something. But, except for Joy, there wasn't anyone.

I reached the outskirts of the city, and I'm afraid I wasn't paying the attention that I should have to my driving. I hit a stoplight and sat there thinking and didn't see the light change.

The first I knew of it was when a cab shot past me, with the irate driver leaning out.

"Knothead!" he yelled at me. There were some other things he said, probably worse than knothead, that I didn't catch, and the other cars behind me began an angry honking.

I got out of there.

But now I knew, I thought. Now there was a way. Well, maybe not a way, but at least an idea.

I searched my memory all the way back to the motel and the memory finally came—the name of that other cabdriver, the one who had talked so enthusiastically about hunting coons.

I drove into the courtyard and parked before the unit and sat there for a while trying to get it figured out.

Then I got out of the car and walked to the restaurant. In the phone booth, I hunted up the name of Larry Higgins and dialed the number.

A woman's voice answered and I asked for Larry. I waited while she went to call him.

"This is Higgins speaking."

"Maybe you remember me," I said, "and again you mightn't. I'm the man you took to the Wellington Arms last night. You were telling me about hunting coons."

"Mister, I tell everyone who'll listen about hunting coons. It's a passion with me, see."

"But you didn't just tell me. We talked about it. I told you I hunted ducks and pheasant and you asked me to go coon hunting sometime. You told me—"

"Hey, there," he said, "I remember now, Sure, I remember you. I picked you up outside a bar. But I can't go hunting tonight. I got to work tonight. You were lucky just to catch me in. I was about to leave."

"But I don't—"

"Some other night, though. Tomorrow will be Sunday. How's Sunday night? Or Tuesday. I'll be off on Tuesday might. It's more fun, I tell you, mister—"

"But I didn't call you about hunting."

"You mean you don't want to go? I tell you, once you've done it—"

"Sure, some night," I told him. "Some night real soon. I'll call you and we'll fix a time."

"OK, then. Call me any time."

He was ready to hang up and I had to hurry. "But there was this other thing. You were telling me about this old man who had a way with skunks."

"Yeah, that old geezer is a caution. Honest, I tell you—"

"Could you tell me how to find him?"

"Find him?"

"Yes. How can I get to his place?"

"You want to see him, huh?"

"Sure, I'd like to see him. I'd like to talk with him."

"What you want to talk about?"

"Well . . ."

"Look, it's this way. Maybe I shouldn't have told you. He's a nice old guy. I wouldn't want no one bothering him. He's the kind of fellow other folks could poke a lot of fun at."

'You told me," I said, "that he was trying to write a book."

"Yeah, I told you that."

"And he's getting no place with it. You told me that yourself. You said it was a shame, that he had a book to write but he'd never get it done. Well, I'm a writer and I got to thinking that maybe with a little help . . .'"

"You mean that you would help him?"

"Not for free," I said.

"He hasn't nothing he could pay you."

"He wouldn't have to pay me anything. I could write the book for him, if he's got a book. Then we could split the money we got out of the book."

Higgins considered for a moment. "Well, that should be all right. He won't never get a cent the way he's going at that book. He sure could use some help."

"OK, then, how do I find the place?"

"I could take you out some night"

"I want to see him now if I can. I'll be leaving town tomorrow."

"All right, then. I guess it is all right. You got a pencil and some paper?"

I told him that I had.

"His name is Charley Munz, but people call him Windy. You go out Highway 12 and . . .'"

I wrote down the directions as he gave them to me.

I thanked him when he had finished.

"Call me some other time," he said, "and we'll fix up some hunting."

I told him that I would.

I found another dime and called the office. Joy still was there.

"Did you get the groceries, Parker?"

I told her that I had but that I had to leave again. "I'll put the groceries inside," I said. "Did you notice—was the refrigerator working?"

"I think so," she said. Then she asked, "Where are you going, Parker? You sound worried. What is going on?"

"I'm going to see a man about some skunks."

She thought I was kidding her about the story she had written and she got sore about it.

"Nothing of the sort," I told her. "I mean it. There's an old man by the name of Munz up the river valley. He's probably the only man in the world who makes pets of unadulterated skunks."

"You're kidding."

"No, I'm not," I said. "A gabby cabdriver by the name of Larry Higgins told me all about it."

"Parker," she said, "you're up to something. You went out to the Belmont house. Did something happen there?"

"Not much. They made me an offer and I said I'd think it over."

"Doing what?"

"Their press agent. I guess you'd call it that."

"Are you going to take it?"

"I don't know," I said.

"I'm scared," she told me. "More scared than I was last night. I tried to talk to Gavin about it and I tried to talk with Dow. But I couldn't force myself to. What's the sense of talking? No one would believe us."

"Not a soul," I said.

"I'm coming home. In just a little while. I don't care what Gavin finds for me to do; I'm going to leave here. You won't be gone for long, will you?"

"Not for long," I promised. "I'll put the groceries in the unit and you get dinner started."

We said good-bye and I walked back to the car.

I lugged the groceries into the unit and put the milk and butter and some other stuff in the refrigerator. The rest I left sitting on the table. Then I dug out the rest of the money I had hidden and crammed my pockets with it.

And having done all that, I went to see the old man about his skunks.

35

I parked down at the end of the farmer's yard, the way Higgins had told me to do, off to one side of the gate that led down to the barns, so I wouldn't block the way if someone wanted to come through. There didn't seem to be anyone around, but a smiling, tail-waving, nondescript farm dog came out to bounce around in an unofficial welcome.

I patted him and talked to him a little and he went along with me when I went through the gate and walked through the barnyard. But at the wire gap which led into a field of clover, I told him to go back. I didn't want to take him down to the old man's shack and have him upset a bunch of friendly skunks.

He wanted to argue with me. He indicated that it would be nice the two of us going out into the field, adventuring together. But I insisted that he go back and I paddled his rump to emphasize my words and he finally went, looking back over his shoulder to see if I might possibly relent.

When he was gone, I went across the field, following the rutted wagon road which showed faintly through the stand of clover. Late-fall grasshoppers went scuttering out of the hay as I strode along, making angry whirring noises as they scudded up the field.

I reached the end of the field and went through another wire gap, still following the wagon traces through heavily timbered pasture. The sun was westering and the place was filled with shadows and down in the hollow some squirrels were holding carnival, scampering in the fallen leaves and shinnying up the trees.

The road plunged down the hillside and went across the hollow and up the other slope, perched below a great rock ledge that punched out of the hillside, I came upon the cabin and the man I sought.

The old man sat in a rocking chair, an old, rickety chair, that creaked and groaned as if it were about to fall apart. The chair rested on a little area that had been leveled off and paved with native limestone slabs that the old man probably had quarried and hauled up the hill from the dry stream bed that twisted down the valley. A dirty sheepskin pelt had been thrown over the back of the chair and the skinned-out forelegs swayed like tassels as he rocked.

"Good evening, stranger," said the old man, unperturbed and calm, as if a stranger dropping in on him were an occurrence of every afternoon. I realized that I probably was no surprise to him, that he had watched me angle down the hillside along the wagon track and come across the valley. He could have watched me all the way and I had been unaware of him, since I did not know where to look to find him.

For now I realized for the first time how the shack blended into the hillside and the rock outcropping as if it were as much a part of this wooded pasture landscape as the trees and rocks. It was low and not too large and the logs of which it had been built had weathered until they were a neutral tone that had no color in them. A washstand stood beside the door. A tin washbasin and a bucket of water, with the handle of a dipper protruding from it, stood upon the bench. Beyond the bench was a pile of firewood, and the blade of a double-bitted ax was stuck in a chopping block.

"You are Charley Munz?" I asked.

The old man said: "That is who I am. How'd you make out to find me?"

"Larry Higgins told me."

He bobbed his head, "Higgins is a good man. If Larry Higgins told you, I guess you are all right."

At one time he'd been a big man, but he'd been whittled down by age. His shirt hung loose upon a heavy pair of shoulders and his trousers were rumpled with the unfilled look characteristic of old men. He was bare-headed, but his iron-gray hair made it look as if he wore a cap, and he had a short and somewhat untidy beard. I could not make up my mind whether he meant it to be a beard or if he simply hadn't shaved for weeks.

I told him who I was and said I was interested in skunks and knew about his book.

"It sounds," he said, "as if you'd like to squat and talk awhile."

"If it's all right with you."

He got out of the chair and headed for the shack.

"Sit down," he said. "If you're going to stay awhile, sit down."

I looked around, too obviously, I fear, for a place to sit.

"In the chair," he said. "I got it warm for you. I'll pull up a block of wood. Do me a world of good. I been sitting comfortable all the afternoon."

He ducked into the shack and I sat down in the chair. I felt a heel at doing it, but he'd have been offended, I suppose, if I hadn't done it.

The chair was comfortable and I could look across the valley and it was beautiful. The ground was paved with fallen leaves that still had not lost their colors and there were a few trees that still stood in tattered dress. A squirrel ran along a fallen log and stopped at the end of it, to sit there, looking at me. He jerked his tail a few times, but he wasn't scared.

It was beautiful and calm and peaceful with a quietness that I had not known for years. I could understand how the old man could have sat there comfortable through the golden afternoon.

There was a lot to rest one's eyes on. I felt the peace descend upon me and the calmness running through me and I wasn't even startled when the skunk came waddling around the corner of the shack.

The skunk stopped and stared at me, with one dainty forepaw lifted, but a moment later proceeded up the yard, walking very slowly and sedately. It wasn't, I suppose, a particularly big one, but it looked big to me, and I was careful to keep on sitting quietly; I didn't move a muscle.

The old man came out of the shack He had a bottle in his hand, He saw the skunk and cackled into delighted laughter.

"Gave you a scare, I bet!"

"Just for a moment," I told him. "But I sat still and it didn't seem to mind."

"This here is Phoebe," he said. "A confounded nuisance. No matter where you go, she's always underfoot."

He kicked a block over from the woodpile and upended it. He sat down on it ponderously and uncorked the bottle, then handed it to me.

"Talking gets one thirsty," he declared, "and I ain't had no one to drink with in a month of Sundays. I take it, Mr. Graves, that you're a drinking man."

I'm afraid I almost lapped my chops. I hadn't had a drink all day and I had been so busy I hadn't even thought of it, but now I knew I needed one.

"I've been known to drink, Mr. Munz," I said. "I will not turn it down."

I tilted up the bottle and took a modest slug. It wasn't topnotch whiskey, but it tasted good. I wiped the bottle's neck on my sleeve and passed it over to him. He had a moderate drink and passed it back to me.

Phoebe, the skunk, came over to him and stood up and put her forepaws on his knees. He reached down a hand and boosted her up into his lap. She settled down in it.

I watched, fascinated, and so far forgot myself as to take a couple of drinks, one atop the other, getting one up on my host.

I handed back the bottle and he sat there with it in one hand, while with the other he scratched the skunk underneath its chin.

"I'm glad to have you come," he said, "for any reason or for none at all. I'm not the lonesome sort and I get along all right, but even so the face of a fellowman is a welcome sight. But you got something in your craw. You came here for a reason. You want to get it off your chest."

I looked at him for a moment and I made the big decision. It went against all reason and everything that I had planned to do. I don't know why I did it. Maybe the peacefulness that rested on that hillside, maybe the calmness of the old man and the comfort of the chair, maybe a lot of different things had a hand in it. If I'd taken time to think it over, I doubt I would have done it. But something inside of me, something in the afternoon, told me I should do it.

"I lied to Higgins to get him to tell me the way out here," I said. "I told him that I wanted to help you write your book. But I'm through with lying now. One lie is enough. I'm not going to lie to you. I'll tell you the story just exactly as it stands."

The old man looked a little puzzled. "Help me with my book? You mean about the skunks?"

"I'll still help you, after all of this is over, if you want me to."

"I guess it's only fair to say that I could use some help. But that's not the reason you are here?"

"No," I said. "It isn't."

He took a deep drink and handed me the bottle. I took another drink myself.

"All right, friend," he said, "I'm settled and all ears. Get about your telling."

"When I get started," I pleaded, "don't break in and stop me. Let me tell it to the end. Then you can ask your questions."

"I'm a good listener," said the old man, cuddling the bottle, which I had handed back to him, and petting the skunk.

"You may find it hard to believe;"

"Leave that up to me," he said. "Just go ahead and tell me."

So I went ahead and told him. I did the best job that I could, but I was honest about it. I told it just the way it happened and I told him what I knew and what I had conjectured and how no one would listen to me, for which I didn't blame them. I told him about Joy and Stirling, about the Old Man and the senator and about the insurance executive who couldn't find a place to live. I didn't leave out a single thing. I told him all of it.

I quit talking and there was a silence. While I had talked the sun had disappeared and the woods had filled with the haze of dusk. A little wind had come up and it was a chilly wind and there was the heavy smell of fallen leaves hanging in the air.

I sat there in the chair and thought what a fool I'd been. I had thrown away my chance by telling him the truth. There were other ways I could have gone about getting him to do what I wanted done. But, no, I'd had to do it the hard way the honest way and truthful.

I sat and waited. I'd listen to what he had to say and then get up and leave. I'd thank him for his whiskey and his time and then would walk, through the deepening dusk, up the wagon track through the woods and field to where I'd parked my car. I'd drive back to the motel and Joy would have dinner waiting and be sore at me for being late. And the world would go crashing down, just as if no one had ever tried to do a thing to stop it.

"You came to me for help," the old man said out of the dusk. "Tell me what I can do to help."

I gasped. "You believe me!"

"Stranger," said the old man, "I don't amount to nothing. Unless what you told me happened to be true, you'd never bothered with me. And, besides, I think that I can figure when a man is lying."

I tried to speak and couldn't. The words bubbled in my throat and would not come out. I think I was as close to tears as I had been in a long, long time. And within me I felt a surging sense of thankfulness and hope.

For someone had believed me. Another human had listened and believed and I no longer was a fool or crackpot. I had regained, in this mystery of belief, all of the human dignity that had been slipping from me.

"How many skunks," I asked, "could you get together?"

"A dozen," said the old man. "Perhaps a dozen and a half. These rocks are full of them, all along the ridge. They'll be coming in all night to visit me and to get their handouts."

"And you could box them up and have some way to carry them?"

"Carry them?"

"In to town," I said. "Into the city."

"Tom—he's the farmer where, you parked—he has a pickup truck. He would loan it to me."

"And he wouldn't ask you questions?"

"Oh, sure he would. But I could think up answers. He could bring the truck partway through the woods."

"All right, then," I said, "this is what I want you to do. This is the way that you can help "

I told him swiftly what I wanted him to do.

"But my skunks!" he cried, dismayed.

"The human race," I answered. "You remember what I told you . . ."

"But the cops. They'll grab me. I couldn't—"

"Don't worry about the cops," I said. "We can take care of them. Here . . ."

I reached into my pocket and brought out the wad of bills.

"This will pay any fines they'll want to throw at you, and there'll still be a lot of it left over?"

He stared at the money.

"That's the stuff you got at the Belmont house!"

"Part of it," I said. "You better leave it in the cabin. If you took it with you, it might disappear. It might turn back into what it was before."

He dumped the skunk out of his lap and stuffed the money in his pocket. He stood up and handed me the bottle.

"When should I get started?"

"Can I phone this Tom?"

"Sure, any time. I'll go up after a while and tell him I'm expecting a call. When he gets it, he can bring down the truck. I'll explain it to him. Not the truth, of course. But you can count on him."

"Thanks," I said. "Thanks an awful lot."

"Go ahead and have a drink," he said. "Then give it back to me. I could stand a drink myself."

I had the drink and gave him back the bottle and he had a snort.

"I'll start right in," he said. "In another hour or two, I'll have a batch of skunks"

"I'll call Tom," I said. "I'll go back and check to see that everything's all right. Then I'll call Tom—what is his last name?"

"Anderson," said the old man. "I'll have talked to him by then."

"Thanks again, old-timer. I'll be seeing you."

"You want another drink?"

I shook my head. "I have work to do."

I turned and left, tramping down the hillside through the dusk and up the slanting trace that led to the clover field.

There were lights in the farmhouse when I got to where I'd parked my car, but the barnyard itself was quiet.

As I walked over to the car, a growl came from the darkness. It was a vicious sound that brought the hair bristling on my head. It hit me like a hammer and left me cold and limp. It was filled with fear and hatred and it had the sound of teeth.

I reached out and found the handle of the door and the growl went on—a sobbing, choking growl, an almost incessant rumbling torn from the throat.

I jerked the car door open and tumbled on the seat and slammed the door behind me. Outside the growling still went on, slobbering in and out.

I started the motor and switched on the lights. The cone of brightness caught the thing that had been growling. It was the friendly farm dog that had greeted my arrival and had begged to go along with me. But the friendliness had vanished. His hackles stood erect and his bared teeth were a white slash across his muzzle. His eyes were glowing green in the flare of light. He retreated, moving sidewise slowly, with his back humped high and his tail between his legs.

Terror rose within me and I hit the accelerator. The wheels spun, whining, as the car leaped forward, brushing past the dog.

36

He had been a friendly dog and a laughing dog when I first had seen him. He had liked me then. It had taken quite a lot of trouble to get him to stay home.

What had happened to him in a few short hours?

Or, perhaps, more to the point, what had happened to me?

I puzzled on it, while something with wet and hairy feet crawled up and down my back.

Perhaps it was the dark, I thought. Probably in the daylight he was a friendly pooch, but with the fall of night he became the vicious watchdog, setting up a guard for the family acres.

But the explanation had a false ring to it. There was, I was certain, more involved than that.

I glanced at the clock on the instrument panel and the time was six-fifteen. I'd go back to the motel and phone Dow and Gavin to find out what they knew. Not that I expected to find that anything had changed, but to make sure it hadn't. Then I'd phone Tom Anderson and the wheels would begin to turn; for good or bad, the fat was in the fire.

A rabbit ran across the road in front of the car and popped into the weeds in the roadside ditch. In the west, where the dying glow of the departed sun painted the edge of the sky a cloudy shade of

green, a small flock of birds was flying, outlined like blown frag-
ments of soot against the colored sky.

I came to the main highway and stopped, then proceeded out
into the right-hand lane and headed back for town.

The things with wet, cold feet had stopped running on my
spine and I began to forget about the dog. I started to feel good
again about someone believing in me—even if it were no more than
an old, eccentric hermit buried in the woods. Although that old,
eccentric hermit probably was the one man in all the world who
could help me most. More convincingly, perhaps, than the senator
or the Old Man or any other person. That is, if the plan came off,
if it didn't backfire.

The wet, cold feet had stopped, but now I got an itchy ear.
Jumpy, I thought—all tied up and jumpy.

I tried to take a hand off the wheel to scratch my ear and I
couldn't take it off. It was glued there, stuck there, and I couldn't
get it loose.

At first I thought I had imagined it or that I was mistaken—that
somehow I'd meant to lift the hand and then had failed to do it
because of some peculiar lapse of my brain or body. Which, if I'd
stopped to think of it, would have been fearsome in itself.

So I tried again. The muscles in the arm strained at the hand and
the hand stayed where it was, and panic came charging out of the
darkened world to wash over me.

I tried the other hand and I couldn't move it either. And now I
saw that the wheel had grown extensions of itself and had enclosed
my hands, so that the hands were manacled to the wheel.

I stamped my foot hard upon the brake—too hard, I knew, even
as I hit it. But it did no good. It was as if there had been no brake. The
car didn't even falter. It kept on going as if I had not touched the brake.

I tried again and there was no braking power.

But even so, with my foot off the accelerator, even if I had not
used the brake, the car should have been slowing down. But it wasn't
slowing down. It still kept on, at a steady sixty miles an hour.

I knew what was the matter. I knew what had happened. And I knew as well why the dog had growled.

For this was not a car; it was an alien simulation of a car!

An alien contraption that held me prisoner, that could hold me there forever, that could take me where it wanted, that could do anything it wished.

I wrenched savagely at the wheel to free my hands, and in doing so I turned the wheel halfway round and then swiftly swung it back again, sweat breaking out on me at the thought of what a twist on that wheel could do at sixty miles an hour.

But, I realized, I *had* turned the wheel and the car had not responded and I knew there was now no need to worry about what I did with the wheel. For the car was out of my control entirely. It did not respond to brake or wheel or accelerator.

And that, of course, was the way it would be. For it was not a car at all. It was something else, a fearsome something else.

But, I was convinced, it once had been a car. It had been a car that afternoon when the thing that followed me had gone to pieces on the hillside at the whiff of skunk. It had gone to pieces, but the car had stayed there; it had not changed into a hundred bowling balls charging for the swale to gambol in the scent.

Somehow, in the last few hours, there had been a switch— probably in that time I had been sitting at the shack, telling Charley Munz my story. For the dog had not objected to the car when I'd driven in the yard; he had been growling out of the darkness at it when I had returned.

Someone, then, had driven into the farmyard in this car in which I now was trapped, this car which was not a car, and had left it there and driven the actual car away. It would not have been hard to do, for when I had arrived there'd been no one around the place. And even, later, if there had been, perhaps such a substitution might have gone unnoticed or, at the very most, occasioned only some mild wonderment for someone who was watching.

The car had been real to start with; of course, it had been real. For they probably had guessed that I would go over it and perhaps they had been afraid that I might have been able to spot some wrongness in it. And they couldn't take the chance, for they had to have a trap for me. But once I had examined it, once I'd convinced myself that it was an actual car, then, they must have reasoned, it would be safe to switch it, for having once satisfied myself, I'd have no further doubt.

Perhaps they had limitations and were well aware of them. Perhaps the best that they could do was to ape externals. And perhaps, even then, they had certain blind spots. For the car I had wrecked with gunfire on the road had its headlight in the middle of the windshield. But that had been, of course, a quick and sloppy job. They could have done much better, and perhaps they knew they could, but there still might have been a doubt about their competence, or perhaps a fear that there were ways they did not know about in which a bogus car might be identified.

So they had played it safe. And playing safe had paid off. For they had me now.

I sat there, helpless, frightened at my helplessness, but not fighting any longer, for I was convinced that no physical effort could free me from the car. There might be other ways, short of physical, and I tried to think of how I might go about it. I might, for example, try talking with the car—which sounded silly on the face of it, of course, but still made a kind of sense, for this was not a car but an enemy which undoubtedly was very much aware of me. But I shrank from doing it, for I doubted that the car, which probably could have heard me, was equipped to answer. And carrying on a one-sided conversation with it would have been akin to pleading, in which the words I said would seem to be disregarded with a disdain that would spell out humiliation. And I, despite the situation in which I found myself, was not reduced to pleading or to humiliation.

I felt regret, of course, but not regret that touched upon myself. Regret, rather, that my plan would not go through, that now nothing would be done, that the one slim chance I'd had to beat the aliens at their game must now be lost by default.

We met other cars and I shouted at them, hoping to attract attention, but the windows of my car were closed, and I suppose the windows of the other cars were closed as well, so I was not heard.

We went for several miles and then the car slowed down and turned off on another road. I tried to figure where we were, but I'd lost track of landmarks and I had no idea. The road was narrow and crooked and it wound through heavy woods and here and there it skirted great humps of rock that shouldered out of the contour of the land.

Watching the roadside, I guessed, rather than recognized, where we might be headed. I watched more closely after that and became convinced that the guess was right. We were going to the Belmont house, back to where all of this had started, where they would be waiting for me, grim-lipped, perhaps, and angry—if things like these could be grim-lipped and angry.

And this was the end of all of it, quite naturally. This closed out the chapter. Unless, of course, there might be someone else, perhaps in some other place, who was working on the problem—and working alone because no one would believe him. It was, I told myself, entirely possible. And where I had finally failed, he might somehow succeed.

I knew, in the back of my mind, just how slim the chance of such a thing might be, but it was the only hope I had, and in a moment of fantasy I grabbed it close and held it and tried to make it true.

The car swung round a curve and did not quite make the curve, and ahead of us was a picket fence of trees. We were hurtling toward them, and the wheels came off the road. The car began to tilt, nose downward, as it took the dive.

Then, suddenly, there was no car and I was in the air alone, in the darkness without a car around me, flying toward the trees.

I had time for a single scream of terror before I hit the tree that seemed to come rushing at me through the dark.

37

I was cold. There was a cold wind blowing down my back and it was dark—so dark I couldn't see a thing. There was a chill dampness underneath me and I was sore all over and there was a dismal sound, a strange keening coming from somewhere in the dark.

I tried to move, and when I moved I hurt, so I quit moving and just lay there, in the chill and dampness. I didn't wonder who I was or where I was, for it didn't make much difference. I was too tired and I hurt too much to care.

I lay there for a while and the sound and dampness went away and the darkness closed in on me, and then, after a long time, I was me again and it still was dark and even colder than it was before.

So I moved again, and again it hurt me, but when I moved I reached out my hand, with the fingers open—reaching, seeking, grasping. And when the fingers closed, they closed on something that I recognized, something soft and pulpy that I squeezed inside my hand.

Moss and fallen leaves, I thought. I'd reached out into the darkness and my hand had grabbed moss and fallen leaves.

I lay quiet for a moment, letting where I was soak into me—for now I knew I was somewhere in the woods. The keening noise was the sound of wind blowing in the treetops, and the dampness underneath me was the dampness of woodland moss, and the smell was the smell of woods in autumn.

If it had not been for the cold and hurt, I thought, it wouldn't be so bad. For it was a pleasant place. And I hurt only when I moved. Maybe if I could suck the blackness inside of me again, it would be all right.

I tried, but the darkness wouldn't come, and now I was beginning to remember about the car that had gone hurtling off the narrow curve and how the car had gone away and left me all alone, flying through the dark.

I am alive, I thought, aghast that I should be alive—remembering the tree that I had seen or sensed and that had seemed to come rushing out of the dark at me.

I opened up the fingers that had grabbed the moss and leaves and shook my hand to get rid of them. I put out both my hands to raise me up. I moved both my legs, pulling them beneath me. Both my arms and legs worked, so there was nothing broken, but my belly was a mass of soreness and there was a pain that went skittering through my chest.

So they had failed, after all, I thought—the Atwoods, the bowling balls, whatever one might call them. I was still alive, and I was free of them, and if I could reach a phone, there still was time to carry out my plan.

I tried to stand, but I couldn't make it. I pushed myself to my feet and stood there for an instant while waves of pain washed over me. My nerve gave out and my knees folded and I slid to the ground and sat there, with my arms wrapped around me to hold in the pain that threatened to burst out.

I sat there for a long time and the edge of the hurt was dulled. It remained as a leaden lump of misery that settled somewhere in my middle.

Apparently I was on some sort of steep hillside and the road must lay above me. I had to reach the road, I knew, for if I could reach it, there would be a chance that someone would come along and find me. I had no idea how far it might be up to the road—how far I had been thrown before I hit the tree or how far I might have rolled or slid once I hit the ground.

I had to reach the road, and if I couldn't walk there, I'd have to creep or crawl. I couldn't see the road; I couldn't see a thing. I existed in a world of utter darkness. There were no stars. There was no light at all.

I got to my hands and knees and started creeping up the hill. I couldn't go far at a time. I seemed to have no strength. I didn't seem to hurt as much as I had before, but I petered out.

It was slow going and hard going. I ran into a tree and had to creep around it. I got entangled in a clump of what I took to be blackberry bushes and had to crawl some distance along the hill before I could bypass them. I came to the moldering trunk of a fallen tree and managed to claw my way over it and keep going.

I wondered what the time might be and felt along my wrist to see if I still had my watch. I did. I cut my fingers on the broken crystal. I held it to my ear and it wasn't ticking. Not that it would have done me any good if it had been, for I couldn't see it.

From far off I heard a murmur, different than the moaning of the wind blowing through the treetops. I lay still and strained my ears to identify it. Then suddenly it was louder and unmistakably a car.

The noise served like a goad and I scrambled madly up the hillside, but the mad scrambling was only motion mostly. It did little to speed up my progress.

The noise increased, and to my left I saw the blur of light thrown by the oncoming machine. The light dipped and disappeared, then appeared again closer.

I began to yell—not words, just yelling to attract attention—but the car swept around the curve above me, and no one seemed to hear me, for it kept going on. For an instant the light and the rushing body of it filled the horizon above the hill, and then it was gone, and I was left alone, crawling up the slope.

I closed my mind to everything except getting up the slope. There would be, sometime, another car coming along the road, or the one that had passed would be coming back.

After a time—it seemed to me a long time—I finally made it.

I sat on the shoulder of the road and rested, then carefully got on my feet. The hurt still was there, but it didn't seem as bad as it had been before. I was able to stand up, not too solid on my feet, but still able to stay standing.

It was a long way I had come, I thought. A long way since that night when I had found a trap set before my door. And yet, thinking back on it, the time had not been long perhaps no more than forty hours or so.

And in that time I had played a futile game of chess with the thing that had been the trap. This night the game was meant to end, for I should be dead. The aliens, undoubtedly, had intended that I should be killed and at this moment, more than likely, believed that I was dead.

But I wasn't dead. I probably had a cracked rib or two, and my midriff had taken a beating as it had slammed into the tree, but I was up and standing and I wasn't beaten yet.

In not too long there'd be another car. If I was lucky, there would be another car.

I was hit by a terrifying thought: What if the next car to come along this road should be another fashioned out of bowling balls?

I thought about it and it seemed unlikely. They only turned themselves into things for a certain purpose and it would not be reasonable to suppose they'd need a car again.

For they did not need a car to travel. They had their burrows for that. Through them they could travel from whatever place they were to anywhere on Earth and, more than possibly, from one place to another on the Earth. It was not too imaginative, I told myself, to envision the space occupied by Earth as laced and interlaced with a vast system of their burrows. Although I realized that "burrows" was, perhaps, not quite an accurate word.

I tried a step or two and found that I could walk. Perhaps, instead of waiting for a car, I should start walking on the road, out toward the main highway. There I would be sure of picking up some help. The rest of the night might pass upon this road without another car.

I went limping down the road and it wasn't bad except that my chest was sore and pains went shooting through it at every step I took.

As I walked, the night seemed to grow a little brighter, as if a heavy bank of clouds had broken and was moving out.

I had to stop every now and then to rest, and how, as I did, I glanced back the way I'd come and saw the reason for the light. A fire was burning in the woods behind me, and, as I watched, the flames shot up with a sudden gush, to leap into the sky, and through the redness of the glare I saw the shape of rafters.

It was the Belmont house, I knew; the Belmont house was burning!

I stood and stared at it and hoped to God that some of them would burn. But I knew they wouldn't, that they would be safe within those burrows that led to some other world. I saw them, in my imagination, scurrying for those holes, with the fire behind them—the simulated humans and the simulated furniture and all the rest of it changing into bowling balls and rolling for the holes.

And it was good, of course, but it didn't mean a thing, for the Belmont house was a single camp of them. There were many other camps, in all parts of the world—other places where the tunnels stretched out to an unknown place, the home ground of the aliens. And that home ground, perhaps, was so close, through the science and the mystery of the tunnels, that it was but a second's distance for them to be home.

Two spaced lights raced around the curve behind me and bore straight down upon me. I waved my arms and yelled, then jumped awkwardly to one side as the car rushed past. Then the brake lights burned red holes in the night and the tires were screeching on the paving. The car began to back, reversing rapidly, until it came even with me.

A head stuck out of the driver's window and a voice said: "What the hell? We thought that you were dead!"

Joy was running around the car, sobbing as she ran, and Higgins spoke again. "Talk to her," he said. "For God's sake, talk to her. She is off her rocker. She set fire to a house."

Joy reached me with a rush. She put out her hands and grabbed me by the arms, with her fingers tight, as if she wanted to be sure that I was flesh and bone.

"One of them phoned," she said, and she was choking as she said it, "and said that you were dead. They said nobody could fool around with them and get away with it. They said that you had tried and they had bumped you off. They said if I had any ideas, I better just forget them. They said—"

"What is she talking about, mister?" asked Higgins desperately. "I swear to God she's nuts. She don't make no sense to me. She phoned and asked about Old Windy and she was bawling at the time—but mad even when she was bawling . . ."

"Are you hurt?" asked Joy.

"Just staved up a little. Maybe a rib or two is busted. But we haven't got the time—"

"She talked me into driving out to Windy's," Larry Higgins said, "and she told him you were dead but to go ahead and do whatever you had wanted. So he loaded up a batch of skunks—"

"He did what?" I yelled, unable to believe it.

"He loaded up them skunks and then lit out for town."

"Did I do wrong?" asked Joy. "You told me about the old man with the skunks and you said you'd talked to a cabdriver by the name of Larry Higgins and I—"

"No," I told her, "you did right. You couldn't have done tighter."

I put an arm around her and drew her close to me. It hurt my chest a little, but I didn't give a damn.

"Turn on the radio," I said to Higgins.

"But, Mister, we better be getting out of here. She set fire to that house. I tell you, I had no idea—"

"Turn on the radio!" I yelled.

Grumbling he pulled his head back into the car and fumbled at the radio.

We waited, and when it came the voice was excited: ". . . Thousands of them, millions of them! No one knows what they are or where they're coming from . . ."

From everywhere, I thought. Not just from this city or this nation, but probably from everywhere on Earth, and they had no more than started, for the news would spread as the night went on.

Out on the hillside that afternoon there had been no way in which quick communication could be established, there was no way in which the good news could be spread. For the thing in the shape of a man that had been following me, and the little fractional thing that had been in my pocket in the guise of money, had been far from any tunnel, far from any line of communication.

But how the good news was going out, to all the aliens on the Earth, and perhaps to those other aliens out beyond the Earth, and it had only started now. Before it ended there would be a mountain of them, seeking to share in the ecstasy of this new perfume.

"First there were the skunks," said the excited radio. "Someone dropped a large number of skunks at the intersection of Seventh and State, in the heart of town. No one need tell you what that would be like, with the show and the nightclub crowd.

"Police were told that the skunks were dumped by an old eccentric with a beard, driving a pickup truck. But no sooner had the police begun their hunt for him than these other things began arriving. Whether there is some connection between the skunks and these other things, no one yet can say. There were just a few of them at first, but they have been pouring in steadily ever since they started, appearing in the intersection in steady streams, coming in from all directions. They look like bowling balls—black and about the size of bowling balls—and the intersection and the four streets leading to it now are jammed with them.

"The skunks, when they were dumped out of the truck, were exhausted and confused, and they reacted rather violently against anything which might be close to them. This served to clear the area rather rapidly. Everyone who was there got out as fast as they were able. Cars were piled up for blocks and there were running people everywhere you looked. And then the first of these bowling balls arrived. Eyewitnesses tell us they bounced and skipped and gamboled in the street and that they chased the skunks, The skunks, quite naturally, did some more reacting. By this time the atmosphere in the vicinity of the intersection was becoming somewhat thick. People occupying the cars in the forefront of the traffic jam abandoned their machines and beat a fast retreat And still the bowling balls poured in.

"They aren't gamboling or skipping any more; there isn't room for that. There is just a great, shivering, seething mass of them piled up at the intersection and overflowing down the streets, piling up in front of the jam-packed cars.

"From our position here, on top of the McCandless Building, it is an awful and fear-inspiring sight. No one, I repeat, knows what these things are or where they might have come from or what they might be here for . . .'"

'That was Old Windy," said Higgins breathlessly. "He was the one who dumped those skunks. And, I guess, from the sound of it, he must have got away."

Joy looked up at me. "That was what you wanted? The thing that's happening now?"

I nodded. "Now they know," I said. "Now everyone will know. Now they will listen to us."

"But what is going on?" howled Higgins. "Won't someone explain it all to me? It is another Orson Welles—"

"Get into the car," Joy said to me. "We'll have to find a doctor for you."

"Look, mister," Higgins pleaded, "I didn't know what I was getting into. She begged me to go with her. So I parked my hack and
went. She said she had to find Old Windy fast. She said it was life
or death."

"Take it easy, Larry," I told him. "It was a matter of life or death.
You won't get hurt on this one."

"But she burned that house . . ."

"That was foolish of me," Joy said. "Just a blind striking back,
I guess. Thinking of it now, it doesn't make much sense. But I had
to hurt them somehow, and it was the only way I knew. When they
phoned and said that you were dead—"

"We had them scared," I said. "Otherwise they never would
have phoned. Maybe they were afraid we were up to something
they couldn't even guess. That's why they tried to kill me; that's why
they tried to scare you off."

"The police," shouted the man on the radio, "asks you, please,
not to come downtown. There are tremendous traffic jams and
you'll only add to them. Stay home, stay calm.

They had made a mistake, I thought. If they hadn't phoned Joy,
it probably would have been all right with them. I was still alive, of
course, but it wouldn't have taken them too long to have found out
I was, and then they could have done me in in a proper style and,
this time, without any slipup. But they had panicked and had made
this one mistake, and it was all over now.

A ponderous shadow came loping down the road. A joyful,
happy shadow that pranced excitedly even as it loped. It was big
and shaggy, and out of the front end of it hung a lolling tongue.

It came up in front of us and plumped its bottom in the dust. It
beat the ground with an enthusiastic tail.

"Pal, you did it," said the Dog. "You got them out of hiding. You
exposed them to the world. You made them show themselves. Now
your people know—"

"But you!" I yelled at him. "You are in Washington!"

"There are many modes of traveling," said the Dog, "that are faster than your planes and better ways of knowing where to find a being than your telephone."

And that was right, I thought. For until this very morning he had been with us and then, at sunrise, he had been in Washington.

"Now it's me that's crazy," said Higgins feebly. "There ain't no such a thing as a talking dog."

"Please stay calm," screeched the man on the radio. "There is no need to panic. No one knows what these things are, of course, but there must be an explanation, perhaps a quite logical explanation. The police have the situation well in hand and there is no need to . . ."

"I thought I heard someone," said the Dog, "mention a word like doctor. I do not know this doctor."

"It's someone," Joy said, "who fixes other persons' bodies. Parker has been hurt."

"Oh," said the Dog, "so that is it. We have the concept, too, but ours works differently, no doubt. It is amazing, truly, how many identical goals are accomplished by many different techniques."

"The mass of them is growing larger," yelled the radio. "They are piled up to the sixth-story windows and they reach deep into the streets. And they seem to be coming faster now. The pile grows by the minute . . ."

"Now," said the Dog, "with the mission finished, I must exclaim adieu. Not that I contributed greatly, but it's been nice to visit here. You have a lovely planet. Hereafter you must the better hang tightly onto it."

"But wait a moment," I said. "There are a lot of things . . ."

I spoke to empty air, for the Dog was gone. Not gone anywhere, just gone.

"I be damned," said Higgins. "Was he really here or did I imagine it?"

And it was all right, I knew. He had been here, but now he had gone home—to that farther planet, to that strange dimension, to wherever he belonged. And he'd not have gone back, I knew, if there'd been further need of him.

We were all right now. The people knew about the bowling balls and they would listen now—the Old Man and the senator and the President and all the rest of them. They'd take the needed action, whatever that might be. Perhaps to start with they'd declare a moratorium on all business deals until they could separate the purely human deals from the alien deals. For the alien deals were fraudulent on the face of them because of the kind of money they had used. But even if they had not been fraudulent, it would have made no difference, for now the human race knew, or soon would know, what was going on and would move to stop it: right or wrong, they'd do whatever might be necessary to put an end to it.

I reached out and opened the rear door of the car and made a signal for Joy to get in.

"Let's get going," I told Higgins. "I have work to do. There's a story to be written."

I could see the Old Man's face when I walked into the office. I was already rehearsing in my mind exactly what I'd tell him. And he'd have to stand and listen, for I had the story. I was the only one who had that story and he would have to listen.

"Not the office," Joy said. "We find a doctor first."

"Doctor!" I said. "I don't need a doctor."

I stood amazed, not so much at having said it (for there had been a time when a doctor had been needed), but at my calm acceptance of it, my casual recognition of something that had happened without my knowing of it, and my becoming aware of it so gradually that it caused no wonderment.

For I didn't need a doctor. There was nothing wrong with me. There was no pain in my chest and no soreness in my belly and no wobble in my knees. I moved my arms to be sure about the chest and I was absolutely right. If there had ever been anything broken there, it was mended now.

It is amazing, the Dog had said, in that corny way of his, how many identical goals are accomplished by many different techniques.

"Thanks, pal," I said, looking upward at the sky, just as corny as the Dog. "Thanks, pal. Don't forget to send the bill."

38

Lightning threw the paper on my desk. It still was wet with ink. There were double lines of type across the top of it to bannerline my story.

I didn't pick it up. I just sat and looked at it. Then without touching it, I got up and walked over to the window to look out. There, to the north, was the heaving mountain lighted by batteries of searchlights, well above the skyline now and growing all the time. Hours before all hope had been abandoned of rescuing the radio crew that had been trapped and buried atop the McCandless Building. All that anyone could do now was simply stand and watch.

Gavin came over to the window and stood beside me.

"Washington is talking," he said, "of evacuating the city and dropping an H-bomb on them. It just came on the wires. Wait until the pile appears to stop its growing, then send a bomber over."

"What's the use of it?" I asked. "They're no threat to us now. They were a threat only so long as we didn't know about them."

I walked away from the window, back toward my desk. I looked at my wrist to see what time it was, forgetting that the watch was broken.

I looked at the big wall clock. It was five minutes after two.

The Old Man had been standing beside the city desk, but now he walked over to me and stuck out his hand. I took it and he hung onto it, his massive mitt twice as big as mine. "Good work, Parker," he said. "I appreciate it."

"Thanks, boss," I said remembering that I'd told him none of the things I had meant to tell him. And, curiously, not feeling sorry that I hadn't.

"I've got a bottle in my office."

I shook my head.

He slapped me on the back and let go of my hand.

I walked down the aisle and stopped at Joy's desk.

"Come on, beautiful," I said. "We've got unfinished business."

She got up and stood waiting.

"I intend," I said, "before the night is over to make that pass at you."

I thought she might get sore, but she didn't.

She reached up her arms and put them around my neck, in front of everyone.

You can live to be a million and still never figure women.

ABOUT THE AUTHOR

During his fifty-five-year career, Clifford D. Simak produced some of the most iconic science fiction stories ever written. Born in 1904 on a farm in southwestern Wisconsin, Simak got a job at a small-town newspaper in 1929 and eventually became news editor of the *Minneapolis Star-Tribune*, writing fiction in his spare time.

Simak was best known for the book *City*, a reaction to the horrors of World War II, and for his novel *Way Station*. In 1953 *City* was awarded the International Fantasy Award, and in following years, Simak won three Hugo Awards and a Nebula Award. In 1977 he became the third Grand Master of the Science Fiction and Fantasy Writers of America, and before his death in 1988, he was named one of three inaugural winners of the Horror Writers Association's Bram Stoker Award for Lifetime Achievement

CLIFFORD D. SIMAK

FROM OPEN ROAD MEDIA

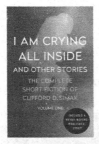

I AM CRYING
ALL INSIDE
AND OTHER STORIES
THE COMPLETE
SHORT FICTION OF
CLIFFORD D. SIMAK
VOLUME ONE

THE BIG
FRONT YARD
AND OTHER STORIES
THE COMPLETE
SHORT FICTION OF
CLIFFORD D. SIMAK
VOLUME TWO

THE GHOST
OF A MODEL T
AND OTHER STORIES
THE COMPLETE
SHORT FICTION OF
CLIFFORD D. SIMAK
VOLUME THREE

ALL FLESH
IS GRASS
GRAND MASTER OF SCIENCE FICTION
CLIFFORD D. SIMAK

Winner of the International Fantasy Award

CITY
CLIFFORD D. SIMAK

ENCHANTED
PILGRIMAGE
GRAND MASTER OF SCIENCE FICTION
CLIFFORD D. SIMAK

A HERITAGE
OF STARS
GRAND MASTER OF SCIENCE FICTION
CLIFFORD D. SIMAK

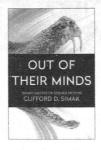

OUT OF
THEIR MINDS
GRAND MASTER OF SCIENCE FICTION
CLIFFORD D. SIMAK

TIME IS THE
SIMPLEST THING
GRAND MASTER OF SCIENCE FICTION
CLIFFORD D. SIMAK

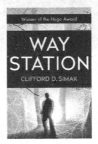

Winner of the Hugo Award

WAY
STATION
CLIFFORD D. SIMAK

OPEN ROAD
INTEGRATED MEDIA

INTEGRATED MEDIA